BREAKDOWN

DARK ROAD – BOOK ONE

BRUNO MILLER

D1372548

BREAKDOWN:
Dark Road, Book One

Copyright © 2018 Bruno Miller

Find out when Bruno's next book is coming out. Join his mailing list for release news, sales, and the occasional survival tip. No spam ever.
http://brunomillerauthor.com/sign-up/

Published in the United States of America.

Do you have what it takes to survive?

Ben Davis was prepared for disaster. He just didn't know it would come so soon.

He and his teenage son, Joel, are miles deep in the backcountry of the San Juan Mountains when high-altitude nuclear electromagnetic detonations light up the pre-dawn sky. Ben, Joel, and their dog, Gunner, must make their way home—or whatever's left of it—on foot.

Without the ability to communicate with his ex-wife in Maryland, Ben has no idea if Joel's brother and sister are okay. The two decide they have no options but to head East. Before their journey begins, they venture into town to check Ben's outdoor store for supplies and discover one of Joel's classmates, Allie, alone and in desperate need of help.

When Ben realizes Allie's flight attendant mother is most likely dead and her father lives in Pittsburgh, he knows he has to take her with them. Ben must use the skills he learned as an Army Ranger many years ago to survive the post-apocalyptic world they now live in.

Can he keep himself and two teenagers safe as they navigate the dark and dangerous road ahead?

For my sister, who encouraged me to write.

· 1 ·

The morning was already well under way by 6:00 a.m. for Ben Davis who was polishing off his second cup of coffee. He enjoyed this quiet time every morning before his son Joel rumbled down the stairs looking for breakfast.

If the weather allowed, Ben would open the rear slider that led onto the deck and wander out to enjoy the view. It was early June, and the mornings were still crisp but warmed quickly, and Ben was very comfortable in a pair of jeans and a flannel shirt. Of course, Gunner, their Chesapeake Bay retriever, always took advantage of the open-door policy.

The dog trotted out onto the deck and down the steps that led to the yard. He did his customary perimeter check, sniffing all the early morning smells before making his way back up onto the deck to find a spot in the sun.

They lived about five minutes outside of

Durango, Colorado, in a little subdivision located on the side of a mountain overlooking town. If you took the dirt road up about three quarters of the way, you would find their house sitting among the aspens and scrub pine at just over nine thousand feet in elevation.

There were about fifty homes scattered across the mountainside although from their house you could only see a few of them. Ben liked it that way. He cherished the privacy it afforded them.

On a clear day you could see all the way through the valley and barely make out a distant mountain range in New Mexico. Most people would find this location quite remote, but not Ben. He would have liked a place a little farther from town with more land, but he was concerned that it would be too far removed for his oldest son Joel to have a social life.

Joel had come to live with his dad after the divorce about five years ago. His younger brother, Bradley, who was ten, and his younger sister, Emma who had just recently turned twelve, lived with their mother in Ocean City, Maryland.

The divorce had been hard on the kids, and it hadn't helped when Joel's mother had moved away with Bradley and Emma. She'd said it was to be near family, but Ben suspected an old boyfriend from her college days was the real reason.

Ben had fought her on it hard, over a year's

worth of time in and out of family court and God knows how much in attorney's fees. Joel was the only one of the three kids that the court deemed old enough at the time to decide for himself which parent to live with.

Ben was sure it had been a bittersweet decision for Joel, but he'd confessed he'd always felt closer to his dad. The countless hunting and fishing adventures they had been on together started at a young age and had no doubt contributed to that feeling. Even before Joel was old enough to participate in the activities, Ben would carry little Joel in a backpack while fly fishing the Animas River, the water splashing up occasionally and tickling at his feet. There were too many good memories like this one for Joel to want to leave.

It was hard on both of them with Bradley and Emma living so far away, and they looked forward to them coming out to Durango for the summer as was their normal routine. In fact, Ben had been hoping to FaceTime with the kids this morning as he did a couple times a week, but he couldn't get through for some reason and resolved to try later on.

Most mornings, Ben made some time to fix Joel a decent breakfast of eggs and bacon or sausage before school, but Joel would have to fend for himself this morning. Something else had Ben's attention, and he'd lost track of time. He had left the slider partially cracked and was listening to the news on the television in the other room while still trying to enjoy the morning from his deck.

The news anchor was talking about how North Korea had successfully tested and proven the effectiveness of their long range missile program recently and how the UN was threatening further sanctions when Joel's footsteps coming down the stairs caught Ben off guard.

He slipped back inside, grabbed the remote and quickly turned off the TV. He normally listened to music in the morning or nothing at all, but this North Korean threat had been occupying way too much space in his mind lately. Things had been escalating for quite a while now and it seemed that it was coming to a head.

Still, there was no need to worry Joel unnecessarily. Besides, the boy had better things to think about, like their fishing trip this weekend. Ben had to get things squared away at the store, too, since they would be in backcountry for a few days and he would be unreachable.

Ben owned an outdoor store in town with an emphasis on fly fishing and backpacking. It wasn't a big place, but they had the essentials anyone would need to gear up for a proper backcountry trip. At one time, he had considered carrying firearms and hunting gear, but the paperwork required to get an FFL (federal firearms license) was long and daunting. In the end, Ben decided it wasn't worth having the government in his business and passed on it.

"Hey, Dad, morning," Joel called out as he headed downstairs. He was in a good mood this morning no doubt because it was the last day of school before summer break. At the sound of his voice, Gunner came running back inside.

Joel shouted, "Look out, Gunner!"

He skipped the last two steps and landed at the bottom of the stairs nearly crashing into Gunner, who was waiting impatiently to greet him. Ben knew Joel considered Gunner his dog. Ben had gotten the dog for him as a puppy right after his mom moved away. He'd hoped it would ease the pain and help Joel cope with his siblings and mother moving. Joel had bonded instantly with the puppy and they'd been inseparable ever since.

"Sorry, but you're on your own for breakfast today. I lost track of time this morning," Ben said as he began to clear a spot on the table for Joel to eat. Ben had been cleaning one of his pistols on the table the night before.

It was a desert tan Glock 19 that he planned on taking with them camping this weekend. The gun was only a 9MM and not the biggest caliber pistol he had, but it was lightweight. The gun was also one that Joel could handle with proficiency as well, should anything ever happen to Ben.

Ben always carried a gun while camping, just in case, and in the last six months or so had started to conceal carry on a more regular basis. He often had cash from the store on him at night if he didn't get a chance to make a deposit at the bank, and he thought better safe than sorry. Some parts of town had really gone downhill in the last year or so, it seemed, and he didn't want to risk it.

"Don't worry about it. I'll just grab something and take it with me." Joel was already closing the fridge door with a banana and an orange juice in his hand.

"You're in a hurry today. What's the rush?" Ben asked.

Joel dropped his head and rolled his eyes. "Yeah, well, I've gotta pick up Brian and give him a ride because his piece of junk isn't running. Again."

"I'm sure he appreciates it, Bud," Ben said.

"It would be nice if he appreciated it with a little gas money," Joel said with a smile, and laughed a little at his own joke.

"I hear that."

"Oh, and Dad, after school today a few of us might go up to Lemon and hang out if that's okay with you? You know, last day of school and all." Joel looked hopeful.

"Yeah, okay, just remember you still have to pack your backpack for the trip. And we're bugging out early tomorrow morning," Ben said.

"I know. I got it. No worries. I won't be home late, promise," Joel said sincerely.

"All right, Buddy. Well, have a great last day. Love you," Ben said.

As the door closed behind Joel, Gunner sat and watched through the glass in the door and would remain there until Joel drove out of sight. Ben thought for a moment about turning the TV back on, but he hesitated and decided not to.

"Nope, got to keep moving. Can't get sucked into that today and waste time," he said to Gunner.

Time was something he wasn't going to have a lot of today. But the real reason he didn't want to hear what the news anchor had to say was because he had heard it all before.

North Korea had been in the news daily for quite some time now. Ben had done his own research as well out of curiosity. It seemed the most intelligent theories he read were of the opinion that the greatest imminent danger from North Korea would be a HEMP bomb. HEMP was an acronym for high-altitude nuclear electromagnetic pulse.

Basically, it was a missile with a nuclear payload that would be detonated at a high altitude. The higher the detonation the bigger the radius of affected areas. The effects of a HEMP attack could literally reach out for thousands of miles depending on the altitude and power of the nuclear burst.

He'd also read that back in 1962 the U.S. government had conducted tests in Hawaii under the code name "Project Starfish." It had been a small HEMP detonation at a low altitude and it had adversely affected electronic devices over 800 miles away. Experts believed North Korea was successfully making the nuclear weapons but lacked the ability to consistently launch the missiles and put one over a specific target for detonation.

He'd learned most of this information by doing his own research and reading, but these were just the basics and there were many unknowns about the potential damage that could result from a HEMP or multiple HEMP strikes. Unfortunately, he'd found limited answers to his questions online, with much of the information being classified or not available to the public.

All this weighed heavily on his mind at times. He worried for the future of his children. He hoped and prayed that his kids would know a peaceful life and never have to face the awful things they spoke of on the news.

But if things did go south, he knew at least Joel would be equipped to handle most situations. Ben was doing his best to pass on all the skills the military had taught him as an Army Ranger, and Joel was a quick study.

If the world did come to an end, Ben and his son would be prepared.

· 2 ·

The clock moved so slowly, it was almost painful.

Then again it was hard to believe that when that minute hand reached the six, Joel's junior year of high school would be officially over. At 3:30, summer would begin.

It had been a good year overall and, like most kids, Joel was focused on the immediate future, which for him, meant the quarry.

He was so focused, he hardly noticed his friend Brian throw a wadded up piece of notebook paper at him, trying to get his attention. "Dude, what's up," he whispered.

"You're not going to chicken out, *are* you?" Brian asked.

"I'm committed, man. I'm doing it."

The unofficial plan was to meet up at their cars in the parking lot after school let out. Not that he needed a reminder since that was their usual daily routine after school, but today was to be a little different. Joel had agreed with Brian and a few friends to head to the local reservoir and take *the plunge* as it was known among upperclassmen or those soon to be. It was a matter of pride and, to Joel's inner circle of lacrosse teammates, a rite of passage.

The speaker sounded with the final computerized chime. That sound had always reminded Joel of what prison must be like. Until today.

Finally the school year was over and they were all free.

Joel quickly navigated the room with his sparsely loaded backpack, making his way to the door.

His English teacher, Mr. Valdez, caught his eye for a second and blurted out, "Read something this summer."

"Yes, sir," Joel gave him a respectful nod and darted out of the room into the hallway. Truth was that Joel planned on reading up on one particular thing this summer, something he had already been researching for quite some time already, and that was how to prepare himself for entry into the Navy.

Even more specifically, the Navy SEALS.

He had been fascinated with the Navy SEALS since he was a young boy. Both his father and grandfather had been in the military, and he felt it was his path to continue that tradition.

Joel cruised right past his locker on the way to the parking lot, no need to stop as he had cleaned it out the day before in anticipation of a hasty exit today.

As he rounded the corner of the gym building on the backside of the school that led to the student parking lot, he laid eyes upon his 1972 K5 Chevy Blazer. It was very easy to spot, considering it stood several inches above the other vehicles in the parking lot thanks to the four-inch suspension lift he and his dad had just installed a couple months ago.

This truck was a labor of love for him and his father. They had found it online some years back before Joel even had his license. Being the perpetual planner that he was, Joel had decided what he wanted to drive at an early age and spent many hours researching and locating "The One."

His dad was good with mechanical things so they'd agreed to fix up something Joel could afford. They had painted it a simple dull tan not unlike the military vehicles Joel had drooled over as a kid. It made sense primarily because it was cheap, since they could do it themselves, and it was a good match with all the hunting and fishing they did. There were never any worries about scratching it on any of the mountain trails they were on.

With the black rims and utilitarian appearance, it could easily be mistaken as a military vehicle.

Joel was very proud of his truck. Because of how easy it was to spot, it had become the after school gathering place for Joel and his closest friends. Somehow Brian was already there talking with a couple girls that had recently taken notice of the truck since the lift.

"Hey guys. Brian, you ready? Today is the day."

"Let's do it, man," Brian responded.

Joel knew better. For a couple weeks now, Brian had been apprehensive about the jump.

"You guys are crazy," the girls said in unison.

That only stoked Brian's machismo. "It's no big deal," he said. "I'm ready."

Joel played along to his advantage. "Outstanding!"

He felt like a dork for saying that but saw that Allison grinned. Allison Young was one of the girls hanging around his Blazer. Allie, as she was known at school, was a good-looking, athletic blonde that had caught Joel's eye when she transferred to their school as a sophomore last year. She had moved from the East Coast somewhere, and no matter how hard he had tried, he'd never worked up the nerve to talk to her.

Yet here she was, standing at his truck in the student parking lot, talking to him.

"How about you?" she asked, looking in Joel's direction.

"Yeah, I'm going to do it. All the juniors playing

varsity lacrosse next year have to do it sometime this summer. I figured, why not today?"

"Getting it over with early, huh?" she asked.

"I guess so," Joel said.

"Well, we might just have to come and see for ourselves. Maybe we'll see you guys up there." Allie gave Joel a quick little smile as the girls turned and walked way.

Joel's heart beat faster in his chest as he realized that the stakes had just been raised on an already daunting challenge.

"Dude! Snap out of it! You look like you're in a trance. Be a little more obvious why don't you?" Brian laughed as he gave his friend a hard time.

But Joel knew it was no secret he'd taken an interest in Allie since she'd moved here. It was no secret either that he'd never worked up the nerve to talk to her or ask her out. He changed the subject.

"Come on, let's get going. I need to stop and fuel up, and you're giving me ten bucks for gas this time," he said, trying to put the focus on his friend.

After putting gas in the Blazer and grabbing a couple energy drinks, which Brian insisted would help them get up the nerve to jump, they headed out of Durango on Route 240 towards Lemon Reservoir.

It was about a twenty-minute drive that slowly ascended into the San Juan Mountain range at about ten thousand feet. The last several miles were dirt road. Lemon Reservoir was a manmade feature with a surface area alone of over 622 acres. It was surrounded on all sides by reddish limestone cliffs eroded into the sides of the mountain valley in which it sat. The water level in the reservoir could change by as many as sixty inches depending on the amount of snowmelt from the previous winter. It had been a cool spring this year so the winter snowmelt and subsequent runoff had been a little slow and the reservoir was close to winter levels.

The dirt road around the south side of the reservoir wound along the edge for about four or five miles ending at a campsite and more dirt roads that meandered up into the mountains. When the water was low, one end of the reservoir had a lower side that resembled a beach and was a popular spot for fishing as three or four small streams converged and dumped directly into it. Joel had been there fly fishing many times for rainbow trout and brown trout, and in the right season there was a Kokanee salmon run.

Being up here got him thinking about the upcoming backpacking trip with his father tomorrow. It had become a tradition of theirs ever since his mom and dad had divorced. It was a good way for him and his dad to bond and share their common interests for the outdoors.

Joel was quickly reminded why they were there

as he pulled around the bend in the road and saw Allison's blue Jeep parked at the trailhead. "She must have passed us when we stopped to get gas," Joel said. He and Brian hopped out of the truck and started the half mile hike into the spot where they would be jumping. The trail ran along the edge of the reservoir and as they approached, they could see down to the water from several spots on the path.

"Water's pretty low, man," Brian remarked.

Joel had already noticed that on the drive in. The trail was a narrow dirt footpath that led to what was originally known as a great photo opportunity spot with an almost panoramic view of the entire reservoir. It was actually a large boulder that stuck out from the mountainside, creating the overhang.

From there, a slender stream ran across the trail and around the boulder making a small waterfall that dropped straight down from the rock, exaggerating the erosion and causing a deep pool at the bottom directly under the boulder.

"We were beginning to think you weren't coming." He heard Allison's voice as they came into view.

"We had to make a quick stop at the store on the way," Brian said.

Joel wandered over to the edge and glanced down into the deep pool below. Brian followed him over and looked, too. Joel figured the drop was about fifty feet down in reality, although it sure looked a lot further.

The dark reddish-brown water that was probably in the upper forty-degree range at best didn't make it any more inviting.

Brian let out a sigh and was about to say something when they heard a clucking noise that turned into laughter coming from the bushes behind them.

Danny Whitman strutted out of the woods and asked, "What's a matter, chicken?"

Joel shot back, "We just got here, Danny."

Danny Whitman was a boy that Joel didn't particularly care for. He was a showoff and a loudmouth as far as Joel was concerned, and he was a constant annoyance on the lacrosse field.

Joel had really been hoping he wouldn't come to the reservoir today. Having Allie here was nerve-wracking enough. The last thing he needed was "Danny the Instigator" in the mix. Now he probably wouldn't get a chance to talk to Allie like he had hoped.

Allie rolled her eyes, visibly irritated at Danny's antics. "I don't see you jumping, Danny!"

"Oh, I will. Don't you worry about it," he said. "As a matter of fact, why don't you jump with me?" Danny said, grabbing Allie by her arm and pretending that he was going to pull her over the edge.

"Knock it off, that hurts!" Allie scolded, swatting at where his hand had grabbed her arm. Danny pulled away too quickly to avoid being struck, causing Allie to shudder backwards toward the edge. Joel lunged at Allie, catching her already outstretched hand, and pulled her back away from the edge to safety.

"You're an idiot, Danny!" Joel shouted.

"Oh, relax. She was fine, she was nowhere close to falling. I was just fooling around," Danny said, looking a little worried himself at how close she had come to the edge but trying not to show it.

"Yeah, well that was really stupid," Joel said.

Allie was rubbing her arm where Danny had grabbed her. A red mark in the shape of Danny's fingers was slowly appearing on her forearm.

Joel's anger rose up inside him, making his hand close into a fist. Maybe what Danny needed was a punch square in the jaw.

· 3 ·

Brian, in hopes of defusing the situation, interjected, "So Danny, did you come here to jump or just to irritate everyone?"

With that, Danny took his keys and phone out of his pockets, rolled them up in his towel and tossed them under a nearby tree. He turned around immediately and took a few long strides past the others that launched him off the rock and up a couple feet. As he jumped, he spun around in the air and extended his right arm and shot everyone the finger as he began to fall.

Joel's dad had once explained this gesture to him as an indication of one's IQ, and Joel certainly agreed in this situation. Danny was a moron. All the same, Joel, Allie, and Brian ran to the edge to watch Danny's plunge.

"He better pull his arm in tight before he lands—" Joel wasn't finished talking before Danny hit the water with the offending arm and finger still extended. A loud smacking sound echoed up the rocks.

Danny surfaced seconds later howling. "Ow! Help, I'm hurt." He grimaced in pain. "Seriously, I'm hurt, something's wrong with my arm!" he shouted up.

The others thought he was kidding around at first, trying to play them all for fools. As they watched, though it became apparent that Danny had in fact hurt himself and was having trouble swimming to the edge of the pool and safety. Joel couldn't believe it.

"Are you kidding me? Unbelievable," Joel said.

"What are you going to do?" Allie asked.

"I guess I'm going to have to help his sorry butt." Joel sighed.

He tossed Allie his keys and phone from his pockets. "Hold those." She nodded, and with that he turned and took a big step off the jutting rock. Joel was sure to tuck his arms in tight to his body and keep his legs straight with toes pointed downward.

He hit the near freezing water like a knife. It instantly overloaded his senses like a thousand cold needles stabbing at him. He opened his eyes a little before he made the surface, but in the dark cold water he couldn't see a thing.

Two good breaststroke-style pumps and he broke the surface. With an audible gasp, he took a big breath. Danny was about ten feet away and still struggling. Joel made his way over to him and grabbed Danny under his good arm, across his chest and brought his hand up to the opposite shoulder.

"Be careful, my arm hurts bad. I think it's broken." Danny was shivering and starting to look pale.

Joel worried he might be going into shock. He had to get them both to the bank fast. As Joel swam toward the pool's edge, a loud splash erupted behind them.

Joel glanced back. Brian had followed Joel over the edge as soon as it was clear to jump. Brian caught up to them and helped Joel get Danny to the edge and drag him out onto the bank.

They all sprawled in the sand for a bit panting and trying to catch their breath. Danny coughed up some water he had swallowed. He rubbed his injured arm, holding it bent at the elbow tight against himself, moaning a little.

Just as they were getting up and composing themselves, Allie came running down the trail that led down in a switchback pattern from the top where they had jumped.

"Are you guys all right?" She panted, half out of breath herself.

Brian looked at Joel and then at Allie and said, "We're fine." Then they looked at Danny, who was sitting on an old log near where he had been lying.

"But I don't think he's doing too good," Joel said. He had a feeling they were all thinking the same thing. That Danny had gotten a taste of karma. But just looking at him, sitting there in pain, no one wanted to call him out on it.

"Sorry guys," Danny said sheepishly.

"Did you break it?" Brian asked.

"I don't think so, I can still move it. Maybe it's sprained." He extended his arm out a few inches, bending it at the elbow while he grimaced a little.

"I need to get home," he muttered. "My dad is going to kill me."

"I think you're pretty lucky that's all you did," Allie said.

"It doesn't feel very lucky," he whined as he started shuffling in the direction of the path back to the top.

The others shook their heads and followed him up the trail. Nobody spoke much on the way to the trailhead and when they got there, Danny gathered his things and headed to his car without saying another word.

"Hey!" Joel shouted, stopping him.

"What?" Danny asked.

"You okay to drive?"

"I'll survive." With that, Danny slinked out of sight, down the path towards the parking area.

"That was really nice of you guys to help him out like that." Allie was looking at Joel.

"Well, the guy's a jerk, but I couldn't let him drown. No choice really." Joel shrugged.

"You know, just your average everyday hero stuff," Brian quipped.

They all laughed a little.

Allie held out Joel's phone and keys. "Here's your stuff, Joel. I took the liberty of putting my number in your phone in case you want to get together sometime over the summer."

Excited, embarrassed heat rushed through Joel's muscles. He hoped his nerves didn't show. He did his best to act calm. "Yeah, that'd be great, I'd like that a lot."

Allie twirled a strand of blond hair around her finger. "If you're working at your dad's store again this summer, you could always stop by and say hi after work sometime. My house is only a few blocks away over at 401 East Seventh Street."

"Cool," was the best response Joel could manage.

Allie turned and walked away slowly spinning around once more for a second to face Joel. "Hope to see you around, Joel. Bye, guys." Then continued her spin and headed towards her car.

"Bye." Joel wanted to say something more, but he was tongue-tied and kept quiet for fear of saying something that might sound stupid.

"Well, I guess I won't be seeing much of you this summer." Brian rolled his eyes.

"Oh, shut up, man. She's hot and you know it. But seriously, come on. I've got to get going." Joel tried to change the subject. It was getting late, and the sun was shifting behind some of the taller mountains, casting a shadow on the boys.

Suddenly, they realized how cold and wet they were and raced for the truck. On the ride home they made small talk about summer plans. Brian was going to visit his aunt and uncle in California for a few weeks. He'd be flying out super early on Sunday so Joel wouldn't see his friend again until almost July. They made some loose Fourth of July plans before Joel dropped Brian at his house.

Joel said goodbye, only half paying attention. He was still in disbelief at how the afternoon had unfolded. He felt like his truck was floating on a cloud or maybe it was him. It had turned out to be a great afternoon. Much better than he ever could have hoped, actually.

Allison Young had asked him out more or less, he was leaving on a backcountry fly fishing trip with his dad in the morning, and his brother and sister would be there in a week or so. This was going to be a great summer.

No, this was going to be the *best* summer. Nothing could ruin these next few months.

· 4 ·

Joel pulled into the driveway around seven. He had about an hour to himself before his dad got home a little after eight. As he parked his truck, he could see Gunner waiting at the glass French door that led into the mudroom off the kitchen. His tail wagged so hard his whole body shook.

"Hey, dog!" Joel was greeted at the door with wet kisses from Gunner and some jumping. He wasn't supposed to greet people by jumping on them, but training had proved useless and they'd given up long ago. Gunner quickly ran to the bottom of the steps and relieved himself before he raced back up to the deck to continue his greeting.

Gunner was ready to love just about everyone, but occasionally there would be someone that he wouldn't take to. He showed his distrust by grumbling about it just loud enough to let you know. He was very protective of Joel and had earned the nickname, Velcro-dog from Ben because

24

he seemed to be stuck to the boy whenever possible.

Joel rummaged through the fridge for leftovers and found some pizza that would make do for dinner tonight. He knew his dad would stay at the store until closing, wanting to make sure everything was taken care of before they left for their trip.

With Gunner in tow, Joel jogged upstairs to his room to start organizing his pack. As he was going through his camping and fishing gear, his mind kept wandering to thoughts and feelings about Allie.

He had already talked himself out of texting her several times, not wanting to seem too desperate. He turned up the music in his room a little as if it was going to help him focus on the trip.

He went through his fly boxes and took inventory. He tied some of his own flies off and on, but it was delicate work. Besides, it was too easy to grab them out of the bins at his dad's shop where there were hundreds of sizes and styles to choose from.

Continuing through his checklist, he made sure he brought his MSR Guardian Military-Grade Water Purifying hand pump. This device was one of his prized possessions, given to him as a Christmas present last year from his dad.

With it, Joel could turn any water source into clean potable water. The siphoning tube had a weighted end that you could toss out into deeper water that led up to a lever style pump handle. The whole thing resembled an old-fashioned well pump, but in a miniature version. You mounted the contraption to a 32-ounce Nalgene water bottle, and it would fill with clean drinkable water in about thirty seconds. That made it possible to only carry the water you wanted and save room in your pack while reducing weight.

Other items he made sure to include were his sleeping bag and pad, and a lightweight two-man tent. His dad would pack his own two-man tent, that way they each had their own, allowing plenty of space to pull their gear in with them at night. Gunner always ended up in Joel's tent anyway, so it was nice to have the extra room.

As he was putting the last few items in his bag, he noticed Gunner's head come up off the floor and look in the direction of the driveway. Dad must be home. The dog always knew when either Ben or Joel was approaching even before they could be seen or heard coming.

Ben steered his Jeep onto the last section of gravel road that led to their house, startling a fox in the road with his headlights as he rounded the turn. He slowed to let the animal cross.

Satisfied that he had prepared the staff to handle anything that might arise in his absence, he finally started to feel himself relax a little as he turned into the driveway. Now he could focus on the trip tomorrow and spend some quality time with Joel. They didn't get to fish or hunt together as much as they used to, so Ben treasured these trips where they could tune out the world and escape the day-to-day responsibilities they had both become accustomed to.

"I'm home!" Ben called out as he entered the house. He survived Gunner's wet and wild greeting and headed into the kitchen. He unloaded his work bag onto the counter with a contented sigh and put his coffee mug from the morning in the sink.

Ben called again, up the stairs this time. "I'm home, Joel!"

Sometimes Joel would have his headphones on if he was playing with Bradley on the Xbox. Ben wasn't crazy about him playing a lot of video games but didn't mind at all when Joel included his brother in an online game. He was grateful for this aspect of modern technology that allowed them to stay connected. The thought reminded Ben that he wanted to try to FaceTime the kids tonight before it got too late.

"I already ate and I'm just finishing putting my pack together!" Joel shouted from upstairs.

"Okay, well I stopped at Bread on the way home and got some of those big oatmeal cookies to take on the trip, but I thought you might want one tonight. Maybe later?"

Joel popped his head around the hallway at the top of the stairs. Bread was the name of a bakery and deli in town that was one of his favorite places to eat. Their soft chewy thick oatmeal cookies were about the size of Joel's hand, and he couldn't pass them up especially if they were fresh. It was big enough to be practically a meal by itself and was more of a cross between an energy bar and a cookie.

"I'm coming, hang on," Joel said.

Ben smiled a little. He could always get Joel's attention when there was food involved.

Joel came down the stairs and headed right for the fridge to pour himself a glass of milk.

"How was the last day of school?" Ben asked.

"Pretty good. Glad the year is over. I'm so ready for summer," Joel said with relief.

"Did you guys make it up to Lemon after school and take the plunge?" Ben asked.

Joel seemed a little surprised. "Uh, yeah we went up there after school." He immediately took a big bite of cookie that even Gunner would have had a hard time swallowing, hoping to buy some time in the conversation.

"I was young once, too, you know," Ben said

with a grin. Joel's answer had been kind of indirect, but he got that his son might not want to go into the details of what they'd done. "It's okay, I know things," he chuckled.

Joel looked a little embarrassed, looking down sheepishly after being called out.

"You know Danny Whitman?" Joel asked. "He plays attack position on my lacrosse team."

"Yeah," Ben said.

"He didn't make out so good today up at Lemon. He hurt his arm when he jumped. Brian and I had to help him out of the water."

"That sounds pretty brave of you guys." Ben had a feeling Joel was leaving out the heroics, but it was a small enough town. Ben would hear the details sooner or later. "I'm sorry to hear he got hurt. What happened?"

"I don't know, I guess he landed wrong. You know Danny, always showing off. Anyway, it was no big deal. He drove himself home, so it probably isn't that bad." Joel shrugged. "Brian and I made the jump without any trouble, but you know we used common sense. Something Danny lacks," Joel was quick to add.

"Well, I hope he's okay. It wouldn't be much fun spending the summer with your arm in a cast, would it?" Ben asked, implying that it could have been Joel that was hurt. "Let's not make a habit out of the plunge thing, okay?"

Joel guiltily nodded. "Yes, sir, I won't, just a one-time thing."

Ben and Joel talked for a while at the table, mostly about tomorrow's adventure but a little about Joel's future and his desire to join the military. Time flew by and when Ben looked at his watch, it was approaching eleven.

"All right, Buddy, that's it for me tonight. And I suggest you get some sleep as well. Six a.m. is going to roll around before you know it, and I definitely want to get out of here early and capitalize on the day."

"Yeah, I'm gettin' kind of tired myself."

"Good night, love ya," Ben said.

"Love you, too." Joel made his way up the stairs to his room.

Ben finished tidying up and got ready for bed himself. He felt very satisfied to finally lie down in bed and have the day behind him. He ran through a quick checklist in his mind and confirmed everything was ready for their trip. Now if he could only quiet his mind, he could get some much needed rest. News blurbs from a radio show he had listened to earlier in the day echoed in his head.

The insults and threats had been lobbed back and forth for years now between the U.S. and North Korea. There was nothing unusual about that, but things had seemed to escalate in recent months with North Korea's nuclear capability increasing steadily. The previous U.S. administration had made many promises of action if they pursued a nuclear program but failed to act on them. Meanwhile the North Korean regime had done just that and recently been successful at detonating a 50-kiloton-plus bomb that greatly enhanced their confidence. They lacked a delivery system capable of reaching the U.S. at this time, as far as anyone knew, but claimed to be developing that technology. As of yet, they hadn't managed to prove those capabilities beyond a few smaller missiles and one nuclear-capable Hwasong-12 intermediate-range missile that ended in the Sea of Japan. The Hwasong-12 ICBM (intercontinental ballistic missile) flew only half of its capable range. Missile defense systems in both Japan and the U.S. failed to intercept the ICBM. Although it was not carrying a payload, it was one step closer to presenting a direct threat to the U.S. Ben knew it was only a matter of time and wasn't sure how it would all turn out, but he was certain this high stakes game of chicken was bound to end poorly.

The last thing Ben recalled was looking at the dim light of his bedside alarm clock, excited for tomorrow. Too tired to think about anything else today, he drifted off.

Ben rubbed his eyes as he sat up in bed, there was still time before the alarm went off but he decided to get a start on the day, anyway. He enjoyed a little extra time in the shower. This would be his last for a few days and he wanted to extract the full benefit of the hot water and steam as it eased his muscles.

Once he got dressed, he hauled his pack out to the mud room and set it by the door. He shuffled back into the kitchen and started a pot of coffee so he could concentrate on making them a good breakfast. He checked the time and figured he would let Joel sleep another ten minutes or so while he loaded the Jeep.

When he came back in he was glad to see Joel at the table eating breakfast with his pack at the bottom of the stairs.

"Morning," Joel said.

"Good morning," Ben replied. "I thought I would have to get you up this morning."

"Not a chance. I want to get going as soon as we can." Joel's eyes lit with excitement. "I can't wait to get up there today."

Gunner impatiently paced back and forth from Joel at the table to Ben in the kitchen. He could sense that this was no ordinary morning. All the activity and gear being packed meant that they were all going somewhere. Even Gunner had his own doggie backpack that Ben filled with dog food and treats for camping trips such as this.

Ben loaded Joel's gear in the Jeep while he finished his breakfast. He also made sure the house was locked up except the front door and double checked that Joel's truck was locked. They never had any problems with theft in this neighborhood, but they would be gone for a couple of days and Ben wanted to be certain.

Joel and Gunner came out the front door. Joel stopped on the landing and looked at his dad. "You got everything? Want me to lock it behind me?"

"Yep, that's everything," Ben replied. "Lock it. We're ready."

Joel secured the door, then hustled to the Jeep. He opened the passenger door and Gunner launched himself into the truck and quickly occupied the front before Joel had a chance to.

Ben laughed.

"Um, do you mind dog?" Joel hooked his thumb toward the rear of the Jeep. "Get in the back, Gunner."

With a woof, Gunner repentantly turned and hopped onto the rear bench seat where he made himself comfortable.

Ben shook his head. Gunner had tried to reclaim his right to ride shotgun shortly after Joel had gotten his driver's license and always rode in the front with Ben when it was just the two of them.

He cranked the engine and they took off, headed to a trailhead just above Vallacito Lake. The drive would take about an hour, mostly because the last ten miles or so were narrow dirt roads.

Midway around the lake they turned off onto a Jeep trail and went another five miles to the Los Pinos River trailhead. From there they would continue their journey on foot.

Ben parked, they got their gear out, and he locked up the vehicle. They put their packs on, Gunner included, and headed up the trail for a few miles until they reached a spot where the river forked and then merged back together after a few hundred yards around a large grassy area that formed an island.

The river ran shallow on one side and was pretty easy to wade across. Gunner led the way with reckless abandon, splashing water everywhere, then abruptly stopped and waited for them on the opposite bank while they hobbled over the loose river rock and balanced against the current.

The water was cold and clear, not yet clouded by silt from the winter melt at this altitude. The vegetation was sparse but showing signs of recovery from a long cold winter. This spot was far enough up trail to escape the casual day hikers and occasional fly fisherman.

Once they were situated on the island, they would be concealed from any passing hikers that did make it up this far. By the time they settled in at the campsite they were well over twelve thousand feet in elevation. There were thousands of great places to fly fish around Durango, but this place had a comfortable familiar feeling to them and was their own little slice of heaven.

Ben let Joel decide on the place to set up their tents. He found a nice level spot on the far side of the island and they quickly unburdened themselves of the nearly fifty-pound packs. Joel unclipped Gunner's pack and let it fall to the ground.

Gunner seemed as relieved as they were to have arrived. He trotted down to the river a few yards away for a drink.

"Dad, you want to see if anything's biting?" Joel asked.

"After I get squared away here, I'm going to go round up some firewood, and while I'm doing that maybe you can catch us some dinner." Ben grinned at Joel. He knew his son was anxious to assemble his four piece backpacking fly rod and get his line wet, but tent setup came first.

"I'm on it." Joel said.

As soon as Joel had finished with his tent, he quickly assembled his fly rod and threw his fly fishing lanyard around his neck.

"Let's go, boy." Joel patted Gunner's head as he started towards the river.

"Have fun," Ben said.

"I'll be back with dinner." He stuffed one of his fly boxes into his shorts pocket.

Ben watched his boy for a moment, pride filling his chest. It didn't get any better than this. This trip, and the memories they'd make up here, were why he worked so hard. Some days were tough, but today made it all worthwhile.

This was a trip they would never forget.

· 5 ·

Joel headed down river for about a quarter mile and fished his way back upstream, casting to every pool and slack water along the way.

He noticed a fish rise several yards upstream and across the nearly twenty-yard wide section of river. There was a hatch of caddis flies going off, so Joel quickly tied on an elk hair caddis that he figured for a good imitation and crouched down as he cast to the spot.

The fly drifted lazily downstream for a few seconds before the water exploded in an eruption of foam and bubbles. The slack line in his right hand flew through the rod guides until all the slack was gone. The rod tip bowed down and trembled from the struggling fish. The trout launched itself out of the water in protest of becoming dinner. Joel could see that it was a nice size and would probably be enough for both of them along with the MREs they had brought along.

Gunner rushed out into the river up to his chest and watched the action excitedly.

"Gunner, back up, boy, come on!" Joel called, trying to get Gunner out from between him and the trout as he waded deeper holding the rod tip up and trying not to break the trout off the line. Eventually the fish tired, and Joel was able to coax it in close enough to scoop it up in his net.

"Woohoo, look at that, will you, Gunner! Now, that's what I call dinner," Joel shouted over the rushing water he was standing in as he looked down at a fat brown trout in his net. Normally, they practiced catch and release fishing, but when they were backcountry, they made an exception for the occasional fish over the legal size.

Eager to show his dad the trout and realizing the sun was beginning to cast shadows across the river, Joel headed back to camp to show off his catch and get it cleaned for dinner.

He marched into camp with the trout held high above his head. Gunner strained his nose to smell the air.

"Well, look at that." Ben nodded at the catch. "That's a nice looking fish you got there."

"Put up a pretty good fight," Joel boasted. "It inhaled an Elk Hair caddis down by the big boulder."

"Oh yeah, that pool there has always been a good spot," Ben said. "That can be a tough spot to work. Good job!"

Joel strolled to the water's edge to gut and clean the fish while Ben opened up a couple MREs and started to prepare dinner.

When Joel returned with the fish, Ben wrapped it in foil with a little salt and pepper and placed it on a hot rock at the edge of the fire. It only took about five minutes to cook before he pulled the fish off the rock using a couple sticks. Everything always tasted better when they were camping, and the trout was no exception.

The two were silent for a while as they enjoyed their dinner. After they finished eating, they split a Hershey bar and lounged around the fire talking about life and Joel's plans for the military after he graduated next year. They talked for a couple of hours as they stared up at the stars until Ben felt his eyes growing heavy and thought it best to call it a night.

"Well, that's it for me." Ben stood up, arching his back and yawning. The trek up might not have worn out Joel, but Ben was feeling it.

"How far do you want to hike up the river tomorrow? Are we going to check out that little creek, the one that runs off towards Granite Peak?" Joel asked.

"Yeah, I think we should. We never got to check that out last time we were up here. Should be pretty good fishing down in that canyon. It's worth the hike."

"Sounds good, I'm going to bed too then, if we're hiking in that deep first thing in the morning." Joel headed for his tent. Gunner stayed by the fire. "Lazy dog!"

Ben unzipped his tent and climbed in backwards, sitting down first. He took off his boots at the threshold before carefully placing them inside the corner of the tent. He climbed the rest of the way in getting comfortable and began to zip up the fly when he paused just long enough to look at Joel about to head into his tent.

"Good night, Buddy, sleep tight."

"Good night, Dad. See you in the morning." Joel unzipped his tent.

Gunner, on hearing the tent zipper, reluctantly got up from his spot near the dwindling fire and made his way into the tent ahead of Joel. "Well, help yourself why don't you, dog." Joel snorted.

Gunner found a spot to his liking at the foot of Joel's sleeping bag where he curled up and seemed to fall asleep almost instantly, ignoring Joel's comment.

Joel took off his boots and climbed in the tent and straight into the sleeping bag. He pushed his feet down alongside Gunner, grateful for the warm spot the dog had already made. He took one last look at the stars before zipping up his tent and lying back in his bag.

Gunner was already quietly snoring in contentment. Joel rolled his eyes. His thoughts quickly turning to dreams as he blissfully drifted off to sleep thinking about tomorrow's adventures and maybe a little about Allie. He wondered if she was the outdoorsy type. He thought maybe she was. She'd come up to Lemon to watch them take the plunge, after all.

Would she ever want to go fishing or camping like this? Some girls were grossed out by that kind of thing and didn't like getting dirty, but he really hoped Allie was different.

When they got back from their trip, he was definitely calling her.

Maybe they would hit it off and she would end up being his girlfriend. He smiled, eyes closed, thinking about the possibility.

Him and Allie. Boyfriend and Girlfriend. Wouldn't that be a way to spend the summer? Better yet, wouldn't that be a great way to start his senior year?

· 6 ·

Ben wasn't sure if he was dreaming or if he'd actually heard something as he rubbed at his eyes. In fact, he thought he'd felt something, more so than he believed that he'd heard something. There it was again. He was awake, and the deep, earth-moving rumble that he heard and felt was real. Then he noticed a dim orange light filtering through the tent material, enough to cast faint shadows across things in the tent.

"Hey, Joel!" Ben called out, simultaneously grabbing his shoes and unzipping the tent.

Joel didn't respond.

"Joel, get up. Come on, get out here." Ben made his way to his feet slowly. He remembered sleeping on the ground used to hurt a lot less in his younger days.

Squinting upward he scanned the sky in the direction of the red-orange glow as he got his bearings and noticed that the clear night sky from earlier now seemed to be obscured by a sort of haze.

"Northeast" Ben said to himself, realizing Joel hadn't answered him yet. Just then, Ben heard a zipper and turned to see Joel's head peek out from behind the tent flap.

"What's going on?" Joel asked, still very much asleep, and unlike Gunner, who was wide awake and pushed his way out of the tent past Joel through the small opening.

"I'm not sure," Ben said calmly, not wanting to alarm Joel.

Just then another explosion to the south, this time much closer. Out of their tents, both of them now had a clear view. A bright orange flash overwhelmed the valley for a split second as Ben threw up his hand to cover his face from the sudden blast of light.

"Don't look at it!" Ben shouted.

A deep bass rumbled up the valley and momentarily canceled out all other sound, followed a few seconds later by a warm breeze the likes of which Ben had never felt in the mountains before. The bright flash of light had diminished to a pale orange glow that seemed to be floating within a distant massive cloud that consisted of an ominous column of fire and blackness that reached well up into the atmosphere where it became encircled by a giant orange glowing ball of fire and smoke mixed with what seemed like lightning.

They both stood there watching in silence for what felt like an eternity before either one of them said anything. *This can't be happening,* Ben thought to himself, *they actually did it.*

"Dad, uh, what's going on? What is it?" Joel asked.

"Son, I think we just witnessed a nuclear explosion," Ben said solemnly. "I'm just guessing, but I would say that last one was over Vegas or maybe Albuquerque and the one before it that I caught the end of when I came out of the tent looked to be in the direction of Denver. I... I... I think they're EMPs, Joel. High altitude nukes." He ran his hand through his slightly graying brown hair.

"Well, what are we going to do?" Joel said in disbelief.

"We're going to pack up our stuff and get home as quickly as possible and then plan our next move from there," Ben said, almost machine-like.

Realizing how he probably sounded to his son he took a couple steps towards him and put his arm around Joel as he pulled him close.

"We'll figure it out, we'll be all right. We have enough supplies at home to last a long time and even more down at the store if we need them." Ben hoped he sounded reassuring to his son, because he wasn't sure he believed his own words.

"Do me a favor and check your phone to see if it's working, and I'll do the same," Ben asked, hoping to distract Joel for a moment. They both went to their tents and rummaged through the packs until they found their phones.

"Nothing! It's totally dead!" said Joel.

"Mine too. I had a feeling they wouldn't work. Let me check the emergency two-way radio," Ben answered as he pulled the radio from his pack that was now outside his tent. He turned the power on and began clicking through the channels. Every channel either played nothing but static or no noise at all.

"Useless," Ben muttered.

"But at least it's not dead like the phones," Joel said hopefully.

"Well, from what I know, simple electronics may be functional if they were off at the time of the blast, but anything made in the last decade or so with a computer chip in it will most likely be fried."

Ben looked at Joel and could see a concerned, scared look on his face. "Right now we need to stay focused. Let's get packed up and get off this mountain." Ben gave Joel his best attempt at a reassuring look and a pat on the shoulder before he began to break down his tent.

"Okay," Joel said, clearly still in denial of their situation.

They had their gear sorted out and packed up in about fifteen minutes. During this time, they heard the occasional rumble, although they weren't sure if it was part of the bomb that they had seen just minutes ago or if it there were other bombs being detonated, only further away this time. Ben was pretty sure they were additional detonations but didn't say anything to that effect.

"You ready?" Ben asked, ignoring the distant rumbling.

"Yep," Joel said quietly.

"Let's try to keep a pretty good pace, just let me know if you get tired." Ben looked at his watch. "Almost six a.m., we should make the Jeep by seven thirty or so if we hustle."

"Go as fast as you want, I'll keep up, old timer." Joel smiled weakly, trying to make a joke as he hoisted his pack onto his shoulders and clicked the waist belt in place.

Ben flashed a quick smile in Joel's direction before turning around and marching out of camp. He was glad to see a little enthusiasm in his son and for a brief moment thought maybe they really would be okay after all. That thought was quickly replaced with thoughts of his children who were on the other side of the country in Maryland. Ben had been thinking about them off and on this morning along with a million other things and questions he had about what was really going on all across the country right now. He just hoped Joel wasn't worried about them as much as he was.

The rumbling sounds had all but stopped a couple minutes down the path and now everything seemed eerily quiet with only the nearby river making any noise. Gunner was leading the hike by his usual twenty yards when he suddenly turned around. Facing Ben and Joel as they closed in on him, he seemed to be looking past them and up toward the sky. Gunner tilted his head as a distant whining sound grew louder. Ben and Joel now heard it too. They looked around but were surrounded by a stand of tall lodge pole pines that obstructed their view past several yards in any direction. They couldn't tell where it was coming from. As the sound grew louder it seemed to come from everywhere bouncing off the canyon walls. The noise sounded like what a jet would make as it wound down its engines after landing.

"Where is it coming from?" Joel said loudly so his dad could hear him over the noise.

"I can't tell," Ben shouted.

Gunner began to bark and whine. Just then, a large passenger plane appeared overhead, no longer blocked by the trees. They could tell it was flying way too low, and Ben knew immediately that something was wrong.

Instinctively they both ducked down, although the plane was still several hundred feet overhead and moving at a high rate of speed. The plane was losing altitude quickly. To see a commercial passenger jet this close up in the mountains was surreal and left them both speechless in the moment. The noise began to fade just as quickly as it had come over them as the jet drifted past them on its descent. The engine noise all but gone, the plane seemed lifeless as it banked right, heading down the valley between the two mountains, the same direction the trail was leading them. They watched in silence until it was blocked by the trees once more.

Ben ignored the urge to somehow protect Joel from all that was happening and spoke his mind. "They're going down! We need to head to the crash site and check for survivors!"

They quickened their already fast pace. Ben knew there probably wouldn't be much left of the plane. Landing deadstick at that speed in the mountains would surely rip the plane apart, but he thought it best not to mention that. Ben wondered if all planes were reacting this way mechanically, and for a split second tried to wrap his head around the dismal potential for death and destruction that would be caused by thousands of commercial airplanes losing power and plummeting to the ground. What about the planes that would land in highly populated areas? They wouldn't all land remotely like this.

He was jolted from his thoughts by the sound of steel screeching against rock followed by three explosions, each one louder than the first. Black smoke rose from the skyline beyond the next bend.

"Do you think anybody made it?" Joel asked.

"I don't think so, son," Ben said honestly, realizing at this point there was no sense in trying to sugarcoat anything for Joel's sake. The sooner they came to terms with what was happening, the better they off they would be.

Clearing a large rock at the bend in the trail they came around the corner to find a scene that looked like it belonged in a disaster movie laid out before them. The plane had plowed through pine and aspen trees over a foot around, leaving busted and splintered tree ends sticking several feet out of the ground.

It looked like hundreds of broken pencils sticking out of the ground halfway down the valley separated in the middle by a trench of rock and dirt carved out by the plane's fuselage. It all ended where the river made a sudden turn in the valley. The plane had continued traveling in a somewhat straight line, and what was left of it lay crumpled up like a tin can against the side of the mountain.

The last hundred yards or so were littered with debris of all shapes and sizes. The wings had been ripped off first and had allowed the plane to maintain speed until it was brought to a sudden fatal stop.

"Unbelievable," Ben remarked.

"Wow, it doesn't even look real." Joel coughed.

"Cover your nose and mouth with your shirt, don't breathe that in." Ben pulled the neck of his t-shirt over the lower half of his face as he tried not to inhale the toxic mixture of jet fuel and burnt rubber that hung in the air.

The plane had crossed over the river at one point and left a trail of scraped rock and paint in its wake. As they picked their way through the boulders and plane pieces, Ben noticed a pinkish tint to the water as it foamed up in the ripples of the stream.

"Hydraulic fluid." Ben was disheartened to see the chemicals mix into the river.

"Is that what that is?" Joel asked.

"Yeah. Listen, you wait here and keep Gunner with you. I don't want you getting any of this crap on you. I'm going to get a little closer and check to see if there are any survivors." Ben said, disguising his true motive for Joel staying put. Truth was he didn't want Joel to see the carnage. He anticipated there would be mangled bodies.

"Gunner, come here. Stay." Joel made a motion with his hand and Gunner reluctantly came to him.

Ben picked his way across a narrow section of river using the rocks as stepping stones where he could. Once on the other side, he noticed several streams of fluid running down the riverbank into the water from the wreck. He was amazed that the main body of the plane had stayed together so well. Walking around the side of the tail section he saw the complete crumpled mass. From a distance he thought maybe it had broken into sections but now he could see that it was all here. The once two-hundred-foot-plus long plane had been reduced to less than thirty feet overall from tail to nose upon impact, surely killing everyone on board instantly.

With parts of the plane still on fire and smoking, the heat was almost too much to bear. Ben knew there was no point in getting any closer and backed away in awe of the destruction. Crossing back over the river, he shook his head at Joel.

"Come on, buddy. Let's keep moving. There's nothing we can do for them."

· 7 ·

Even though the trail was mostly downhill on the way back, it was still a challenging hike at the pace they were keeping. They had to stop twice and pump water to replenish their water bottles with Joel's pump, and although it was only a little after eight in the morning the sun seemed hotter than it should be.

The brownish yellow haze that seemed to be floating in the air added to the overall hot, dry feeling. Joel wondered if this was a direct result of the nukes, and how long would it linger.

"How are you holding up back there?" Ben glanced back at Joel.

"I'm good, glad we're almost to the Jeep though." Joel sighed.

"Yeah, should be almost there, a couple more minutes."

Joel recognized this part of the trail and knew his dad was right. They would be at the trailhead parking lot soon. There, they could be free of these heavy packs and have the relative comfort of the Jeep.

Finally, Joel could see the sun glint off the Jeep's front windshield through the trees as they approached the parking area, and he immediately felt a small sense of relief.

They let their packs slide to the ground near the tailgate.

"Ah, that feels good!" Joel said arching his back and stretching.

Ben was already unlocking the driver's side door, not wasting any time, he stuck the key in the ignition and turned it. "Nothing, not even a sound, completely dead." Ben sighed and rubbed the back of his neck.

"You mean we're going to have to walk? Can you fix it?" Joel exclaimed.

"I'm afraid not, the electronics are shot, just like our phones," Ben said. "Relax buddy, I've been thinking about this possibility, and I have an idea. The road out of here is pretty much all downhill until about midway around the lake. If we push the Jeep to the edge of the parking lot where the road starts we should be able to coast down the last couple miles if we're careful. Maybe almost to the main road or at least close to it." Ben sighed.

"I'm game. Let's try it," Joel said, willing to try anything if it meant not having to put his pack back on.

After putting their gear in the back and getting Gunner loaded in, they each took a position alongside the Jeep. With the two front doors open, they pushed the Jeep to the entrance of the parking lot and faced it down the road. Ben pushed the clutch in and slid the shifter back into gear as soon as the Jeep started to roll freely with little resistance.

"All right, let's catch our breath for a minute." Ben huffed and wiped some sweat away from his eyes. "When I throw this in neutral we'll give it a couple good pushes to get going and then hop in, okay?"

"Okay, I'm ready when you are," Joel answered.

"On three then. One, two, three, push!" Ben grunted.

It didn't take much to get the Jeep moving downhill and after only a few steps they both hopped into their seats and pulled the doors closed. They picked up speed quicker than Joel expected they would and before he knew it they were rolling down the road.

It felt good to be sitting down and moving with a slight breeze cooling them down. They actually had to apply the brakes several times during their descent around some of the sharper corners where the road made switchback turns. It didn't take long before they could see the lake coming into view along with the rest of the valley. As they came down out of the high mountains onto the plateau, they could see a much wider view of the horizon.

There were plumes of dark smoke in varying sizes rising up from too many places to count. A few of the plumes were nearby, and some farther off in the distance.

"Look at that! What do you think they are?" Joel asked.

"Could be downed planes, or car wrecks. Hard to say, really. If the nukes wiped out computers and mechanical systems that control the nation's infrastructure, there's no telling what chaos would result from a total breakdown. I'm sure that emergency services are limited at best, maybe even nonexistent." Ben muscled the Jeep around the last slight curve onto the main road around the lake, trying to maintain as much momentum as he could.

Once the Jeep was on the flat dirt road, it slowed quickly and Ben steered it off onto the shoulder where it came to a halt.

"Well, it looks like we're walking from here, better than nothing." Ben climbed out of the Jeep.

"Yeah, I guess so," Joel mumbled.

"Hey! That probably saved us an hour of time. Not to mention it gave us a nice little break," Ben said.

"I know, you're right," Joel said, still sitting in his seat, one hand reaching back to scratch Gunner's ear.

"Look, I know all this is a lot to take in, and it's overwhelming, but just try to take it in a little at a time," Ben pleaded. "Just focus on getting home and try not to worry about anything else right now. I love you, Joel. We're in this together, and we'll get through it together."

"I love you too, Dad. I'm sorry. Let's keep moving," Joel said. With that, he proceeded to get out of the Jeep with Gunner spilling out behind him.

Joel knew they were going to have to walk again, but now it was real as he hoisted the pack back up onto his shoulders. But his backpack wasn't the only thing weighing him down. He felt burdened by heavy thoughts about his friends, his school, Allie, Brian, and most troubling his brother and sister. What did this all mean and how would it affect all these people and things he cared about? It was overwhelming and sad and depressing. He would just have to deal with it as it came and take it one step at a time like his dad told him. He was fortunate to have his dad in all this and he knew it. He knew his dad was tough and had been trained to deal with a lot of things. Joel had always been proud of his dad and his military service with the Army Rangers. But now he was grateful, and in this moment he vowed to be strong for his dad and carry his own weight, without complaint.

After about an hour of steady walking, they

reached the paved road at the bottom of the dam. They hadn't seen any traffic on the road around the lake, not that they were expecting to, but they'd hoped that once they reached the main road, they would see some signs of life.

The landscape was eerily quiet, with no cars on the road and no airplanes in the sky. It was all so still. The haze that floated in the air seemed to filter out some of the sunlight but none of the heat. That combined with the plumes of black smoke scattered across the horizon lent a strange otherworldly feel to it.

Ben stopped and unclipped his waist belt letting his pack slide off his shoulders with a sigh of relief.

"Let's take a minute and top off our water while we're close to the river."

"Sounds good to me." Joel immediately shed the unruly pack.

Glad to take a break, Joel grabbed his water filter and both of their bottles and climbed over the guardrail on the side of the road. Gunner squeezed under the rail and followed Joel down the grassy embankment to the river. Joel quickly filled both water bottles and headed back to the road where his dad had stayed sitting on the guardrail and going through his pack. As Joel climbed back up onto the shoulder of the road, he noticed his dad pulling his Glock out from the pack along with its concealed carry holster. Ben tucked it behind the waistband of his pants just off to one side where it could be easily retrieved while wearing the backpack.

"Thanks for refilling the water bottles," Ben said, noticing Joel was watching him stash the pistol.

"Sure, no problem." Joel paused. "How come you got the gun out of the pack?"

"Just a little peace of mind is all. We're heading into populated areas now, and I just want to be safe. No worries, just a precaution."

· 8 ·

The trio had walked less than a mile before they came to their first driveway. It was a gravel road with a patch of grass running up the middle. The red mailbox out front said *Johnson* in black letters and almost seemed inviting. Having not seen any cars yet, Ben decided they should stop at the house and see if there was anyone home that would be willing to share some information with them. Or possibly they had a working vehicle and could give them a ride. Ben wasn't fond of knocking on a stranger's door in light of all that had happened, but the alternative would be a very long walk home.

"Let's try this house and see if anyone is around," Ben said.

"Maybe they can give us a ride," Joel said.

"Even if they can't, I would be happy to get some information," Ben said, not wanting to get Joel's hopes up about a ride.

As they headed up the driveway, the house came into view. It was a small log and stone cottage set back in a little clearing. If there was anyone home, they would be able to see them coming up the road toward the house. This made Ben a little anxious, but they continued to the house anyway.

There were no vehicles at the house, at least not that he could see.

So much for that ride, he thought.

The closer they got, the more apparent it became that the house was empty. Disappointed, Ben was just about to suggest that they head back to the road when he saw movement in one of the upstairs windows.

There was someone in the house watching them and trying not to be seen.

"Up there in that left top window, I just saw something or someone move, I'm sure of it." Ben scanned for any more movement.

Seeing none, he called out, "Hello, is anybody home? We were camping up above the lake and are just trying to get home."

"Are you sure you saw someone?" Joel asked.

"I thought I did. I don't know. Maybe my eyes are playing tricks on me. I am tired," Ben confessed.

Just then the front door burst open and a boy that couldn't have been any older than ten or eleven marched out onto the front porch brandishing an old double-barreled shotgun. He had the gun on his shoulder and was squinting down the barrel at them.

"My Daddy said not to let nobody in." the boy stammered, red faced and shaking.

"Whoa there, easy kid. We don't want to come in." Ben pushed Joel backwards and behind him. "Is your dad here? Can we talk to him?"

"No, he went to town this mornin' to get supplies. He said he'd be back real soon though, and if anybody came by here messin' 'round, I should shoot 'em."

"Look, take it easy, we're backing away. You can put the gun down. We don't mean you any harm. We're leaving," Ben said as they continued backpedaling through the yard. Gunner growled in protest unsure of what was going on, but backed away with them, nonetheless.

Eventually the boy began to retreat to the doorway and back into the house. Once inside, he quickly grabbed the doorknob and slammed the door shut and just as suddenly as he had appeared, he was gone.

Ben and Joel turned and quickly walked back in the direction of the road.

"Sheesh, that was crazy!" Joel said.

"That was foolish, is what that was. We can't take any more chances like that." Ben was relieved that they had avoided any serious conflict.

"I don't know how long he's been there by himself, but I'm guessing his dad has been gone a while. That poor kid was scared to death." Ben shook his head.

At least now he knew that there were some vehicles that were still running if the kid's dad had driven to town that morning.

"Poor kid, he nearly shot us!" Joel said, interrupting Ben's thoughts.

"He wouldn't have shot us, at least not on purpose. He could barely hold the gun up." Ben looked back at the house.

"Regardless, I'll feel better after we put some distance between us and this place," Joel said.

"Agreed." Ben nodded.

Ben welcomed being back out on the road after their run-in with the kid, and he reminded himself over and over that he would not be that careless again. Joel was counting on him and that could have gone south very quickly. He couldn't take risks like that for Joel's sake.

They continued toward home for several more miles not saying much, both of them engrossed in their thoughts until they approached a spot where the river turned back to run alongside the road for a bit. They found a stand of cottonwoods down by the water that provided some much needed shade and decided to stop there for a while and eat something. They broke out a couple MREs and wolfed down lunch, not realizing how hungry they'd become. After eating, they agreed to stay there for a bit and get some rest before continuing on. They'd been up since at least five that morning, and it had been a long day already. They would wait there until the midday sun passed and it cooled down before continuing on.

Ben was just nodding off when he heard the faint sound of a motor.

"Do you hear that Joel? Listen."

"Is that a car coming? I hear it." Joel said.

They both got up from the grass and made their way to the road, leaving their packs on the ground. Ben hesitated for a second and wondered if they should expose themselves but decided that if there was a chance for a ride home they would have to risk it. They still had at least another twenty miles to go, and a ride would be a huge windfall right now. They needed it.

Once they got to the shoulder, they could see what looked like an older pickup heading in their direction. Ben felt for the gun under his waistband briefly, reassuring himself that this was the right thing to do.

As the old truck approached, he could make out a lone driver wearing a cowboy hat. Ben waved his arm in the air, signaling with the hopes that the driver would stop.

The old brown Ford pickup slowed as it pulled off onto the shoulder toward them. Ben glanced down, making sure his shirt was covering his pistol. The brakes screeched in protest as the truck came to a stop in front of them. The truck, as much rust as it was brown paint, seemed to match the character driving. The old man behind the wheel leaned over from the driver's seat and pushed open the passenger door.

Ben and Joel stepped back a little, unsure of his intentions.

"What are you boys doin' out here? Don't you know world war three's going on right now?"

The first thing Ben noticed was the matte silver .44 Magnum revolver tucked neatly into an ornately carved leather holster hanging off the man's belt. It was hard to miss with its oversized barrel and mother-of-pearl grip gleaming in the sunlight.

The old man noticed Ben's attention to the gun and tried to put him at ease.

"Oh, don't worry about my little friend there. He's just keeping me company on my way into town today. He don't bite... much. Where you fellas headed?" The old man pushed the brim of his hat up with his finger.

"We were fishing up above Vallecito Lake until all hell broke loose this morning. Our Jeep wouldn't start, and we've been trying to make our way home since then, but it's been slow going. I'm

Ben, and this is my son Joel, by the way." Ben reached out to offer his hand and Joel followed.

"Pleasure to meet you boys. Name's Dale, and I'm heading into Durango to check on my son and his family. Phone and electric are out everywhere, and I haven't been able to get in touch with them since this all started," The old man said shaking both their hands.

"What exactly is going on? We've been off the grid since yesterday," Ben asked.

"Well, that's not exactly clear. No mention of anything out of the ordinary news wise yesterday and, of course, this morning we woke up to no electricity or utilities for that matter. There was no warning for what happened this morning," Dale said.

Ben, still feeling the effects of the afternoon sun and the mileage they had covered today, thought he would cut to the chase. "Say, if you're heading into town, do you think you could drop us off at the bottom of Durango Hills?" he asked.

"No problem, glad to help you two out. Grab your stuff and let's go," Dale said.

"Thank you so much!" Ben exhaled deeply.

Faith in humanity restored after their earlier experience that day, Ben and Joel jogged over to retrieve their packs and quickly returned, tossing them into the back of Dale's truck. Ben sat up front on the single bench seat with Dale, and Joel and Gunner climbed into the back of the old pickup.

A couple minutes into the ride, Ben turned to check on Joel and saw that the boy and his dog were both fast asleep. *Good for them*, he thought, *it's been a rough morning.*

Ben's eyes were heavy and the rhythm of the truck could have easily lulled him to sleep also, but Dale seemed intent on telling tales of his good old days on the ranch mixed in with bits of speculation on the cause of this chaos that was now their lives.

But Ben didn't mind the conversation. It still beat walking the last thirty miles to their house, and he was glad they'd finally caught a break.

· 9 ·

Part of Ben wished the ride had lasted a little longer. After the day they were having, it felt good to sit down and let the wind wash over him, the hum of the engine and Dale's stories becoming one at times. It was hard, but he made himself stay awake. He didn't want to take any chances. Dale seemed nice enough, and Ben was very grateful for the ride, but he wasn't letting his guard down again.

Ben's thoughts were interrupted by the squealing of brakes as the truck slowed down and pulled into the Durango Hills subdivision entry.

"This is good here, Dale. You're a lifesaver, really. Thanks a lot," Ben said.

"Sure I can't drive you on up, all the way to your house?" Dale asked.

"No, sir. We don't want to keep you from getting to your family any more than we already have, and our house is just up a little ways. We'll hike up the rest, thank you though." Ben opened his door and climbed out. He leaned back across the seat and shook Dale's hand.

"No problem."

"You be careful in town, you hear, Dale? Things could get ugly once people start to put the pieces together and figure out what's going on. Take care of yourself," Ben said.

"Oh, I'll be all right. This old cowboy's been thrown off a horse or two." Dale winked.

Once Joel and Gunner had unloaded from the back and shut the tailgate, Dale didn't waste any time heading off down the road.

On their own again, they hoisted their packs and headed up the gravel road to their house.

"Too bad he couldn't take us all the way to the house," Joel said.

"Well, he offered, but I told him we would walk the rest of the way." Ben admitted.

"What? Why Dad?"

Truth was, part of Ben didn't want to trouble the old man who had already been so generous, but the tactical side of him didn't want to expose them to an unknown element by showing him where they lived.

"Because Joel, I didn't want to expose us," Ben snapped back. Feeling guilty for raising his voice, he said more calmly, "Dale seemed nice, and he probably is, but this is a different world now, Joel. We have to be cautious who we trust."

"I know I just... I... I'm just tired, Dad," Joel pleaded.

"I know you are. Me too. Hang in there, we're almost home. We'll be sitting down enjoying a hot meal before you know it," Ben said.

As they trudged up the road, Ben couldn't help but think of Dale. He felt sorry for the old man and wondered how people would act towards each other once supplies started to dwindle. He and Joel were going to have to go into town at some point.

He had a lot of supplies and survival gear at his store and he wanted to get to it before someone else did. Maybe not today or even tomorrow, but at some point people would become desperate, and his store would be a prime target for looting. He considered going alone and having Joel stay at the house where it was safe, but he knew the reality of it was that he would need Joel to help him.

"I've never been so glad to see the house before!" Joel said.

"Good job! Proud of your effort today, bud," Ben said.

Joel smiled. "Thanks, Dad." He picked up the pace a little.

The only thing keeping Ben moving forward at this point was the sight of the house and the promise of safety and rest. Gunner bolted for the house with impossible energy and cleared the steps with a single bound only to sit down on the doormat and lean against the door panting as he watched Ben and Joel approach.

With the sun setting, the dark quietness of their house confronted them. The absence of scattered lights from surrounding homes on the mountainside was an ever-present reminder that things were very different now.

Ben headed straight for their little detached garage that sat thirty feet or so off to the side of the house. He unlocked the small side door on the garage then turned to Joel.

"Here, catch." Ben tossed Joel the keys. "After you put your stuff down inside, do me a favor and throw your truck keys out to me, will you?"

"Sure, you think she'll start?" Joel asked.

"If I'm right, yes. Your truck is older, like Dale's, and doesn't rely on a complex computer network running things, just a good old-fashioned electrical system with a carburetor."

Joel unlocked the door to the house and opened it, reaching inside to the wall where they hung their keys.

"I'll do it," Joel said dropping his pack just inside the door and returning with keys in his hand. He unlocked his truck and slid behind the wheel. He pumped the gas pedal twice as he simultaneously turned the key in the ignition. The big 5.7 liter 350 cubic inch V8 roared to life just like it was any other day.

Ben could see the smile on Joel's face through the windshield, and that made everything okay for a moment. Ben thought about all the hours they had spent together fixing up the old truck and how much he enjoyed spending time with Joel doing that. Ben gave Joel thumbs up and then motioned his hand across his throat, signaling him to turn the truck off. The truck seemed extra loud in the darkness, and Ben didn't want to draw attention to their fortune. At least they wouldn't have to hike into town and back. This would give them the edge they needed to get in and get out quickly.

"I'm going to get the generator going. Give it a minute and then get yourself a nice hot shower," Ben said.

A couple years ago he'd had a backup generator installed in the garage. Because of their location, all the utilities were run overhead and were fickle, to say the least, in foul weather. Power outages were common enough to be a major inconvenience, so he'd spent the money and had the generator installed. It ran on natural gas that was piped in from a five hundred-gallon tank located behind the garage.

Ben figured the hot water heater should still work, and because the house was on a well with a large reserve cistern of water, they should be able to enjoy some creature comforts sparingly. And tonight they needed it.

While Joel was getting cleaned up, Ben began clearing a spot in the garage for Joel's truck. He wanted to keep the truck inside and locked up out of sight from any prying eyes. They never parked in the garage, as it had become overrun with gear and kayaks and just about anything else they might need for an outdoor adventure. Ben wondered how they had accumulated so much stuff, as he moved things to the sides of the garage.

Satisfied that he'd made enough room for the Blazer, he stepped outside the building and listened to see how much noise the generator was making. The generator itself was located in the back corner of the garage, but the exhaust ran out through a vent in the rear wall. Funny he never paid attention to how much noise it made in the past. It wasn't excessively loud. Still, he thought they better only run it for short periods when they needed it, just to be safe. With that in mind, he headed inside to get cleaned up himself.

Joel, hair still wet from his shower, was sitting at the kitchen table with a bottle of juice and a box of cereal. Gunner was passed out on the floor next to him, front paws twitching deep in a dream.

"I think the milk is bad. The fridge isn't very cold either," Joel said.

Ben opened the refrigerator and gave the milk a smell.

"I think it's okay, but you should use it up

because it won't last much longer. We're only going to be able to use the generator sparingly. After I get a quick shower, I'm going to turn it off for the night," Ben said, as he walked around to the living room to close the blinds on the front windows. Joel had turned on some of the lights when he came into the house out of habit, and Ben was concerned that someone would see the light coming from inside their house.

"We need to maintain a low profile even when the generator is on. Only use the lights when necessary, okay?" Ben asked.

"Okay. Sorry," Joel mumbled.

"It's all right. It's just going to take some getting used to," Ben said as he headed for his bedroom.

"That's for sure," Joel replied.

"I cleared a spot in the garage for your truck, how about giving me five minutes to get cleaned up then pull it in for the night, turn off the generator for me and lock up for the night?"

"No problem. I can do it, but I'll wait until you're done in the shower," Joel answered.

"Thanks, buddy," Ben said.

Ben knew Joel could handle it. He had gone over the operation of the generator with Joel when it was installed and made sure he knew how to run it in case he was ever home alone and lost power. He was going to have to start relying on Joel a lot more now, and he hoped Joel was up to it.

Although the hot shower felt great, Ben kept it short. Trying to be conservative and also a little anxious to get the generator turned off, he cut it shorter than he would have liked. While he brushed his teeth, the bathroom light flickered and went out. It made him happy that Joel had followed through on what he'd been asked to do. Ben reached over and turned on a small LED lantern that he had brought into the bathroom with him. As he finished brushing his teeth, he stared at himself in the mirror. The LED lantern casting a pale white light up onto his face, he stared at himself in the mirror briefly before snapping out of his fatigue-induced daze. He wanted to talk to Joel a little before they turned in for the night and come up with a battle plan for tomorrow.

As he made his way into the living room carrying the lantern in front of him, he saw Joel sleeping on the couch. Gunner had relocated from the kitchen floor and was curled up on the opposite end of the couch at Joel's feet, snoring away.

Ben didn't have the heart to wake Joel and decided it could all wait until morning. Besides, the kid would need his rest. Tomorrow was going to be another early day.

As Ben laid a blanket over Joel, he considered waiting a day at the house and resting but he was afraid that the situation in town would deteriorate rapidly. Early tomorrow morning at first light would be their best bet for an incident-free trip to the shop and back. They would load the back of Joel's Blazer with all the supplies and gear they could fit and get out of town as quickly and quietly as possible.

Hopefully it wasn't too late to salvage some things, but Ben had no idea what they would encounter tomorrow.

They would go in prepared for the worst.

· 10 ·

Ben was rudely awakened by an enthusiastic and cold nose pressed against his neck. Gunner was nudging him and whining in an effort to get someone to let him outside to do his business. Ben strained his eyes at his watch, pressing the button to illuminate the dial.

"Four thirty, okay. All right. I'm coming," he said to Gunner as he realized he had fallen asleep in the recliner last night.

Gunner scampered to the door, tail wagging.

Ben stood up slowly, still sore from yesterday. He grabbed the small lantern and flicked it on, shuffling over to the door and stretching as he went. He poked his head outside and took a quick look around before he let Gunner out. He left the door cracked enough for the dog to get back in on his own and proceeded to pull out his camp stove and his headlamp from his pack that was still sitting in the mud room from last night.

Might as well get some coffee going and start to get organized for the run into town. He would let Joel sleep a little longer before breaking the news to him of their forthcoming adventure.

Ben put on his headlamp and switched the light on low, not wanting to ruin his night vision while he waited for the coffee to finish brewing. After he poured himself a cup and took a few well-needed sips, he headed to their basement.

Coffee in hand, he made his way down the old wooden steps to the partially finished basement. It was one of his many ongoing projects around the house, and the unfinished basement was one of the reasons he'd been able to get the house at a good price. It had been completely barren when he bought the place.

He had insulated, dry walled, and completed a fully functioning bathroom so far, but still had a little ways to go to finish off the space. He was proud of his progress down here and the way it was shaping up. It was going to be a nice game room for Joel and his friends to hang out once it was completed. At least, that was the plan.

None of that seemed to matter now though. Ben wistfully looked around for a second as he stood at the bottom of the stairs, letting his eyes adjust. His gaze stopped on a stack of hardwood flooring that he realized he may never get to install.

Forcing himself not to dwell on it any longer, he

headed over to the far corner of the main room where the gun safe stood. The safe was the largest model Ben could afford and was rated to hold up to sixty guns. Thankful now that he'd decided on a version with a mechanical lock instead of the fancy electronic option they offered, he spun through the numbers on the dial and turned the lever. The thick safe door swung open to reveal a meticulously laid out mini armory.

Rifles and long guns made a U-shape around the bottom interior of the safe. Some of the guns were old and had belonged to Ben's father. The rifles were organized neatly around six green metal ammo cans stacked on the floor.

Each can held a different type of ammo for the various rifles. On the inside back of the safe door there were a dozen pockets made primarily for holding pistols, but Ben had a few hunting and survival knives in some of the pouches.

Along the right side of the safe were some felt-lined shelves where Ben kept ammo for the pistols and some important paperwork for the business.

On the very bottom was a small wooden box, about the size of a shoebox. This was also something Ben's dad had left him. The box was nearly full with one ounce silver buffalo coins and a variety of others that his father had collected over the years. The last time Ben had researched the coins online he figured there was about four or five thousand dollars' worth of coins in the box. He hoped to be able to pass them on to his kids someday.

Ben was suddenly reminded of the now uncertain future that lay ahead.

Next to the safe was a work bench Ben had planned on removing after he finished the renovation, but in the meantime had become an extension of the safe, holding less important items like hunting gear and bags on the shelves above and below. The main countertop area had become a place to clean and work on the longer rifles. At the end was an old fly-tying vise that Ben had often thought about replacing with his own ammo reloading station. He had done his homework on all that was involved but, regrettably, never got around to setting it up.

Ben grabbed a green double tactical gun case off the upper shelf and laid it open on the counter. He pulled one of the two Olympic AR-15s out of the safe, choosing the one that was set up with the EOTech holographic site paired with a G33 flip magnifier scope. This made the gun suitable for close range targets as well as longer shots when the magnifier was flipped into place behind the holo sight.

He and Joel had just been to the range with this gun and a few others a couple of weeks ago, and it was Joel's favorite gun to shoot. The 5.56 round at 55 grains was consistent, and you could reach out and touch something at eight hundred-plus yards if you needed to and had the skill, but at three to four hundred yards, it was deadly accurate. Ben grabbed another pistol as well, aside from the Glock 19 he was already carrying. He chose another 9MM, a Smith & Wesson M&P model. This way, they would only have to bring two types of ammo and could travel light.

His intentions were to stash the AR in the bag under the rear seat and hopefully leave it there. He wanted Joel to have access to the other pistol. Maybe even conceal it on him. If it went smoothly, he hoped they could be in and out in under a couple of hours. He grabbed some MREs and threw then in a smaller duffel bag along with a couple of extra flashlights and the ammo just in case.

Looking at his watch, he saw that it was a little after five. He figured he should get Joel up so they could get going. He grabbed the bags and scaled the stairs to the living room where he was happy to see Joel already awake. Joel was yawning and rubbing his neck as Ben entered the room.

"How'd you sleep?" Ben asked.

"Okay, I guess. I don't even remember falling asleep last night," Joel answered as he squinted from the light on Ben's headlamp.

"Oops. Sorry about that," Ben said as he turned off the headlamp and parted the living room curtains. The sun was just beginning to provide a modest amount of light and reminded him of the urgency to get moving.

"What's all the gear for?" Joel asked.

"Well, I thought it might be useful for our little trip into town this morning," Ben said.

Joel cocked his head to the side slightly.

"We're going into town?" he asked.

"I'm afraid so. I don't think we'll need any of this stuff, but it's just a precaution." Ben laid the bags on the floor.

Gunner got up from the floor by Joel and sauntered over to give the bags a good sniff, stretching each leg out on the way.

"I want to get down to the store and get all the important stuff out of there before it's too late. I have a pallet of dehydrated food that just came in and is still in the stockroom. We need to grab anything and everything we can. I doubt we'll have another chance to go back anytime soon." Ben sat down on the couch next to Joel. "And besides, we're going to need it if we're going to save your brother and sister," he declared.

"But...but they're in Maryland," Joel stammered, now fully awake.

"I know, but we have no other choice. We have to try. They need us." Ben looked into Joel's eyes. "I have to do this, and I can't do it without you, Joel."

"And I wouldn't let you Dad," Joel said.

Ben smiled and put his arm around Joel as he pulled him close for a second.

"We can work out the details later, but right now let's focus on the task at hand. I'm going to need you to do one more thing for me," Ben said.

"What's that?" Joel asked.

"I want you to carry this." Ben reached into the smaller duffel bag on the floor and produced the M&P 9MM semi-auto and its concealed carry holster.

"From now on, you keep that gun on you at all times, until I say otherwise. Keep the mag full and the chamber empty. Got it?" Ben asked.

"Got it," Joel said with wide eyes.

Joel took the gun from his dad and immediately stood up as he situated the gun and holster onto his belt and behind his waistband. He had worn it before but this time would be different.

"All right, now get yourself something to eat quickly while I take these bags out to your truck," Ben said, grabbing the bags and heading toward the door. Gunner followed Ben outside to the garage, tail wagging.

"I'm afraid you're not going with us right now, boy. Someone's gotta stay back and watch the house," Ben explained.

There was still a chill in the air at this hour, and Ben could see his breath in the garage as he loaded the truck. Gearing up at this hour in the pre-dawn light reminded him of all the hunting and fishing trips they had been on. If only that were the case today. He slid the gun bag with the AR in it under the rear bench seat and unzipped it partway for easy access then covered it partly with an old blanket.

After he had the gear stashed in Joel's truck to his satisfaction, Ben went back into the house to check on Joel. "How's it coming? You about ready?" Ben asked.

"Just about," Joel answered, as he swallowed the last bite of oatmeal cookie left over from the fishing trip.

"I want to leave Gunner here. It can't hurt to have him here to watch the house, plus we need all the room we can get in your truck."

Gunner paced back and forth between Ben and Joel as if he knew somehow that he was not to be included in the morning's activities.

Ben poured the rest of the coffee into a travel mug and grabbed a granola bar. He really didn't feel like eating this morning and was content with just the coffee but knew he should get something down before they left. He was anxious about what lay ahead and it had been a while since he felt these familiar jitters in his stomach.

Those early pre-mission mornings in the Army seemed like a lifetime ago now. Operating in hostile environments was nothing new to Ben, only difference was this time the stakes were higher.

· 11 ·

Ben backed the Blazer out of the garage just far enough for Joel to close the overhead door manually and lock it. Joel then made his way out of the small side door, locking it behind him as well. As he climbed into the passenger seat, he looked back at the house.

Gunner stared longingly at them as they pulled out of the driveway. Joel wondered if Gunner would really deter someone from breaking in. He had witnessed Gunner's aggressive side a couple of times before and thought it was a pretty convincing performance.

Ben navigated the gravel road out of the subdivision slowly, with the headlights off.

"No lights?" Joel asked.

"No, trying to use a little stealth to our advantage. No need to advertise," Ben said.

As they made their way down the mountain, Joel tried to look down the driveways they passed to see if he could spot any signs of life.

All the houses were dark, of course, which he expected, but they seemed different in some other quiet kind of way. There seemed to be a sense of finality hanging in the air. It was hard to describe, but he didn't like the way it made him feel.

Once at the bottom of the road, they made the right onto Rt. 240 and set out for town. As the sun rose higher, Joel noticed random black plumes of smoke here and there. Some were small and faint but others where massive and billowed up into the atmosphere for miles. The closer they got to town, the more there were.

"I guess there are no first responders. Probably have their hands full taking care of their own," Ben said, as if he had read Joel's mind.

"I guess," Joel shrugged.

Joel tried to imagine for a moment what exactly that meant. No firefighters to put out fires or at least keep them under control or from spreading. No police to keep law and order, and no paramedics to respond to medical emergencies. For all he knew there were no medical services available at all. To what level would the government shut down? The local government would almost surely dissolve or be reduced to a skeleton crew. What then? Would the federal government send in the Army or something to maintain order, or were they too busy dealing with North Korea if that was in fact who had sent the EMP nukes? They had just recently talked about some of this in school in his social studies class. Wishing now that he had paid more attention to the boring details concerning the politics, Joel wondered if he would ever go to school again.

Joel's thoughts turned to his brother and sister in Maryland. He hoped they were safe but was very troubled at the thought of them being that far away and only having their mother to take care of them. The thought of never seeing them again briefly crossed his mind, but he pushed it away as he was reminded again just how fortunate he was to have his dad with him. He was certain his dad would figure out a way to get to them and everything would be all right. At least that's what he told himself.

Just then, Joel felt the truck slow a little and looked up from his thoughts to see an awful wreck taking up the oncoming lane and some of theirs. Ben slowed down even more as they got closer and slowly steered them around the two mangled vehicles.

One looked like an older SUV and appeared empty to Joel. The other car was fatally lodged under the bigger SUV and was almost destroyed beyond anything resembling a car. It was all a big melted mess of metal fused together by heat, burned to a black smoldering pile.

As they rolled past, Joel thought he saw what looked like an arm and a hand dangling out of one of the window openings but wasn't sure. He wanted to believe it was something else and resolved not to focus on it.

"That was a bad one." Joel chewed on his lip.

"Yeah, it was. I'm guessing it happened yesterday," Ben said.

"There was hardly anything left of that little car." Joel turned away and tried to focus his attention forward.

"How about helping me keep an eye out? I have a feeling we're going to be seeing a lot more of that kind of thing as we get closer to town," Ben said.

"Okay, will do." Joel shifted in his seat, glad to have a purpose to take his mind off things.

How bad was it going to be in town? What about his friends? Suddenly Joel was overwhelmed with a heavy feeling in his chest as he remembered his best friend Brian had planned to visit relatives in California. How could he have forgotten about Brian? He was supposed to fly out early yesterday morning. Joel remembered Brian telling him he was on the 5:00 a.m. flight to Denver and then getting on another flight from there to LA.

"Do you think all airplanes were affected, what about prop type planes like the smaller planes that fly out of Durango airport?" Joel looked at Ben for a sign of encouragement.

"Yes, probably. Why?" Ben asked.

"Brian. He was flying out early yesterday at 5:00 a.m." Joel winced as he slumped down in his seat.

"I'm sorry, Joel." Ben offered.

"This really sucks." Joel rubbed at his eyes, sniffling.

They rode in silence for a few miles, passing the occasional lifeless vehicle. As Ben navigated through the obstacle course of abandoned cars, Joel's world seemed to speed up, his head flooding with too many thoughts to process all at once. His brother and sister, the plane crash they'd witnesseded, the horrific car wreck they'd seen, Brian and how much he would miss him and all the stupid things they did together, the probability of never finishing school, and the uncertainty of his future in general. Scattered amongst these thoughts was Allie. How could life be so unfair, so cruel? Just when things seemed to be going so well. He'd thought it was going to be a great summer, but all that had changed in the blink of an eye.

Joel slowly regained his composure as he reluctantly accepted their situation once more and took a deep breath. He felt a reassuring hand on his shoulder and looked over at his dad. He had to say something. This might be his only chance if it wasn't too late already. He'd lost Brian, but if there was anything he could do, he had to speak up. He couldn't lose Allie too.

"I met a girl from school." Joel sat up a little in his seat.

"Oh, yeah?" Ben asked.

"Yeah. Her name is Allie. She lives in town not too far from the store, actually right around the corner on East Seventh Street. It's just her and her mom, I think." Joel shrugged.

"Okay. The answer is yes." Ben smirked.

"Yes, what?" Joel pleaded innocently, knowing full well his intentions in bringing Allie up in conversation.

"Yes, after we finish up at the store we can head out of town that way and check on them if you want." Ben shook his head.

"Thanks!" Joel felt a little better to have something to look forward to. It wasn't much, but it was something. He felt desperate to hang on to something from his old life, and his feelings for Allie were a welcome distraction. He had no idea what they would find at Allie's house or what he would even say to her if they found her, but he had to try. He wasn't willing to let go of her that easily, and he wouldn't allow himself to give up on the possibility of salvaging some normality in his life. Hopefully she was okay, but if she needed help, he wanted to be there for her.

Ben noticed the lack of cars on the road, cars that were running that was. The lack of cars was even more obvious now that it was getting light out. The lack of activity and traffic only exaggerated the graveness of the situation.

They neared the end of Route 240 where it turned into one of the main roads into town and came into what should have been a more populated area. Surely there would be some people out and about trying to cope with their new reality. Ben hoped his instincts were wrong and that most people would remain decent and compassionate, like Dale had been to them.

Ben knew firsthand though how chaos and desperation could change people. He had seen his share of atrocities overseas and the aftermath it created while in the Army. The dark side of humanity was very real, and there was no telling what awaited them in town.

The first thing he noticed was a smashed plate glass window at Bread, the bakery where he and Joel had stopped so many times before. Then he realized most of the windows in the small shopping center were broken or cracked.

Black smoke poured from one of the store windows on the other end of the complex. He wondered if people had smashed the windows or maybe the shock waves from the blast. They were much closer now to the location of the last detonation they had seen, although they were probably still pretty far away from ground zero.

The valley opened up here in town as it ran toward the New Mexico border and did not provide the protection of the mountains to buffer the blast. The shopping center looked abandoned except for a few cars in the parking lot, and there was trash and what looked like napkins scattered around on the sidewalk in front of the store. It wasn't like he expected to see the normal morning crowd of cyclists with their bikes lined up out front and a full parking lot of cars, but he wasn't expecting it to look like this after only one day either. He thought he would have at least seen someone by now. They hadn't seen another person since they left the house this morning, but it was still early. Maybe yesterday had been as hard on everybody else as it had been on them. Maybe people were just staying in and keeping to themselves, at least that's what he hoped. Maybe people had left town, but where would they go and how would they get there? The roads were mostly clear except for the occasional cars and trucks stranded in the road, abandoned by their drivers where they stopped running.

The most unsettling thing though was the burned-down houses and buildings they drove past. Some were still fully engulfed in flames while others were little more than smoldering piles of rubble. There were a lot of power lines down and scorched transformers. A massive power surge must have rolled through after the bombs went off. Maybe that had overloaded the circuits and caused a lot of the fires.

The further they drove into town, the more Ben realized how grateful he was that they were in a remote area tucked away in the mountains. It must have been complete pandemonium here when the bombs went off. Hundreds, if not thousands, of people must have died in Durango alone. The sound of sirens and emergency vehicles was expectedly absent, but the eerie silence sent chills up his spine, nonetheless.

Up ahead, a large delivery truck that had been making its early morning rounds had swerved out of control and run into a building, blocking the entire road just after Eighth Street. Ben slowed down to make the turn onto Eighth Street and get around the roadblock. As they passed the jackknifed truck, they couldn't help but notice the slumped over body of the driver in the seat. The front windshield had a red stain over the steering wheel where it had been smashed by the driver's head upon impact, the front of the truck was buried in the building, bricks covering most of the hood from where they had peeled off in a sheet on impact. Ben made the right turn quickly and sped up a little, trying to put it behind them. Trying to minimize the visual for Joel's sake.

They were close now, only a few blocks to go. With a heavy sigh, Ben watched as the buildings and environment seemed to deteriorate rapidly as they got closer to the downtown area and his store.

Pulling onto Main Street, he saw the shops that hadn't sustained damage from fire or vehicles had been vandalized and looted. The situation wasn't looking good. They passed a small Whole Foods store. Both of the front shop windows were broken out and glass was scattered all over the sidewalk. The store looked like it had been ransacked and was now just empty shelves and broken displays.

Ben's heart sunk as he wondered if his store had suffered the same fate.

"It's a little rougher looking than I thought it was gonna be." Ben frowned.

"I can't believe how bad it is." Joel glanced around wide-eyed and mouth open, trying to take it all in.

The condition of the streets rivaled some of those Ben had seen in so many of the unstable third world countries he had been to.

"Hard to accept that it fell apart this fast. I didn't expect things to go south this quickly," Ben said. "I wonder if some of this started prior to the attack, maybe they had some kind of warning. I mean it's only been a day."

"Do you think the store is trashed like these places?" Joel looked at his dad.

"I don't know, but assuming the worst, even if they took everything from the front of the store, I still have a lot of stuff locked up in the back."

Ben's place was one of the smaller shops on Main Street, so he kept a majority of his stock in the back storeroom and mostly just displayed one or two of an item for sale in the storefront. This left plenty of room for a customer to try out the flex of a new fly rod by dry casting or to open up a tent on the floor to help make that sale.

A few years back, Ben's shop had been broken into and vandalized. The thieves had taken a lot of the high-end gear right out of the storeroom where he had the bulk of his inventory. They had backed up to the large roll-up overhead door at the rear of the store in the alley and taken advantage of the neatly boxed items in bulk in the back of the store.

Insurance had covered the loss, but hadn't softened the sting of being violated in such a brazen manner. Ben had decided to invest in a better security system that included a two-hour rated fireproof steel door between the storefront and the back stockroom. In addition to that, he'd added a secondary locking system to the rear roll-up overhead door and the smaller man door next to it.

With any luck Ben's security improvements to the store would prove to be worth every penny today.

· 12 ·

"Okay, here's the plan." Ben leaned in slightly towards Joel. "I'm going to drive by the front of the store and see what we're dealing with first, but then I'll pull down the alley to the rear. I want to get that big roll-up door open and back the truck in far enough to close the door and get out of sight. I'm pretty sure I can get the truck in there, if I angle it a little."

Ben knew it would be a tight fit but was worth the effort to conceal themselves from prying eyes.

"What do you need me to do?" Joel asked.

"I'm not sure yet, but keep your head on a swivel," Ben said sternly.

"Yes, sir." Joel breathed deeply and straightened up in his seat a little.

Ben, satisfied that he had Joel's attention and that his head was in the game, proceeded steadily down Main Street.

His worst fears materialized as he saw years of

hard work reduced to shattered glass and broken displays. One of the glass counter display cases that made up his checkout area was tipped over, its contents of knives, watches and various other outdoor gadgets were long gone. Nothing left but broken parts and pieces of what had once been a source of pride for Ben. Choking back his anger for those responsible for the vandalism, he tried to stay focused. He could see to the back of the shop, and the rear door was still closed and appeared intact.

"Animals!" Ben muttered.

Joel looked at his Dad and then back to the store without saying a word.

"Let's hope the back was spared." Ben turned the wheel sharply pointing the truck down the side street and then into the alleyway that ran behind the row of stores along Main Street. Each shop had its own dumpster in the alley making the alley artificially narrow at each dumpster so it was only wide enough for one vehicle to pass by at a time. As they passed the row of evenly spaced dumpsters on Joel's side of the truck, Ben drove slowly, inspecting each one as they went by.

"I'm just being cautious, don't want any surprises." Ben sensed Joel's gaze on him. To Ben, the dumpsters looked like the perfect place from which to launch an ambush in the narrow alley and his good sense wouldn't allow him to ignore it.

Joel nodded his head.

"The back of the shop looks like it's in good shape," Joel said as the truck came to a stop just past the door.

"I still want you to sit tight for a minute while I make sure it's all clear. In fact, why don't you slide over into the driver's side and get ready to back it in when I open the big door." Ben looked at Joel. "You'll have to back in at an angle. Otherwise, she won't fit."

"I got it, Dad. I can handle it." Joel slid over the console into the driver's seat as Ben got out of the truck.

"I know you can, buddy. Keep an eye on both ends of the alley, okay? And one other thing—" Ben hesitated, thinking.

"What?" Joel questioned.

"Put a round in the chamber of your pistol and then put it back on safety before you holster it," Ben said.

"Okay." Joel nodded.

Ben hoped he wasn't coming off as overprotective, but he knew that the Smith & Wesson 9MM that Joel was carrying would disengage the safety automatically after the slide was pulled back and a round was chambered. You had to manually re-engage the safety, otherwise the hammer would remain cocked and ready to fire. The gun had a featherlight trigger pull weight, which was great for accuracy but could be dangerous if holstered with the safety off. Ben knew that Joel was aware of these things and was confident in his ability to handle the gun. However, Ben also knew that if something were to happen, adrenaline would take over, and he didn't want any accidents.

Ben fished the keys to the rear man door out of his pants pocket and slowly unlocked both locks on the door then quietly slid his keys back into his pocket.

For the second time today he was grateful for his choice of standard mechanical locks. He'd briefly considered electronic locks that had a pushbutton keypad that could even be linked to a smart phone, something the salesman had really tried to sell. In the end though, the electronic locks seemed like more of a liability, and he went with his gut, opting for the more traditional ones.

Ben looked to one end of the alley then to the other, glancing at Joel with a quick nod, he then turned his attention to the doorway. He drew his gun from his waistband then slowly pulled the door open and eased his way in.

He could see the steel door that led to the front of the store and it was definitely closed, but he would proceed with caution nonetheless. Everything seemed to be as he left it in the stockroom. There was a small window in the back wall up high that faced the alley. It wasn't very big but provided enough light to see.

Ben's close quarters battle (CQB) training kicked in automatically as he entered the room, clearing his closest corner then running the wall to the cleared corner scanning the room as he went. His Glock mirrored his glances around the room.

Once he reached the door that led to the front, he checked the handle and confirmed that it was still locked.

Lastly, he made his way over to the small employee bathroom and did a quick check inside to make sure it was empty. Satisfied that the room was secure, he unlocked the overhead door and threw the bolts back on both sides of the doorframe.

When raised or lowered too fast, the door made a terrible racket, and Ben had always hated the noise. Today he was extra careful to lift it slowly trying to retain whatever stealthy advantage they had left. When the door was high enough to allow the truck under it he motioned with his hand for Joel to back up. He was pleasantly surprised how quick and precise Joel maneuvered the truck into the building. Ben held his clenched fist up indicating for Joel to stop backing up. He ran around to the front of the truck and checked for clearance. They had inches to spare.

"Nice job!" Ben nodded in approval.

"Thanks," Joel said.

Ben pulled on the big door and let it down slowly, throwing one of the bolts on the side after it was closed, making sure it couldn't be opened from the outside.

"How about locking that door for me, Joel?" Ben bobbed his head in the direction of the door that he'd first entered through.

"Got it," Joel answered.

When Ben heard the satisfying click of the lock, he felt a small sense relief, knowing that they were at least safe inside the building for the time being while they loaded the truck. *Halfway there,* he thought to himself. *Well, almost, I guess.*

He hadn't figured on stopping by Allie's house. It was against his better judgment to deviate from the plan and, at first, he had regretted telling Joel they could check on them. But, he'd seen the way Joel's expression had changed when he brought her name up, and Ben hadn't had the heart to tell him no. In fact, he'd suggested it in an attempt to capitalize on Joel's improved mood and to take his mind off Brian. It was the first sign of life he'd seen in his son's eyes in a while and he didn't want to squash that. He knew how hard this must be for Joel, especially after being forced to come to terms with the loss of Brian like that. He wasn't exactly sure what they would do if they managed to find Allie and her mother, but they would just have to cross that bridge when they got to it. He just hoped that they were both okay for Joel's sake. He would hate to see his son get hurt again like that today.

Joel lowered the tailgate and opened up the back of the truck while Ben surveyed the tall metal shelves lining the walls filled with boxes of gear.

"So, what are we taking with us?" Joel scooted himself up onto the tailgate and sat down, legs dangling off the back.

"Concentrate on food for now. Let's take all of those Wise company emergency food tubs." Ben pointed to a pallet on the floor.

Joel pushed himself up and off the tailgate with his hands and was at the pallet in two long steps. He began to pull at the cellophane shipping wrap that enveloped the white tubs stacked two high on the pallet.

"Stack them neatly. We're limited on space," Ben stressed.

"I will." Joel rolled his eyes and got to work.

Each square plastic container held 104 servings. They were popular with the backpackers because they were lightweight and only required the addition of water to rehydrate in about fifteen minutes. It was no five-star meal, but it was far more nutritional than canned goods and they were lucky to have them. There were eighteen containers in all, and if Ben's memory served him right there were a couple more canisters back at the house. They would have enough food for months. Maybe they could leave one of the tubs with Joel's friend Allie and her mom if they needed it.

"Here you go." Ben threw Joel his pocketknife. "Keep it. I'll grab another one."

Joel grinned and flicked open the 3.5" Spyderco G-10 blade and made quick work of the thick plastic wrap. He closed the blade, and he admired the knife for a second, rubbing his thumb over the shield and small banner engraved on the handle that read, RANGER 75th RGT.

"Really?" Joel grinned at his Dad.

"Sure, consider it yours. Now quit fooling around and get back to work," Ben teased.

Joel shook his head, laughing as he began lugging the tubs to the truck two at a time. Ben was glad to see the old Joel, even if it was just for a moment.

The dehydrated food would take up a lot of room in the truck but was well worth the space, maybe they should transfer the individual food packets into bags so they would pack better. *Later,* he thought, *at the house. Don't want to be here any longer than necessary.*

"Better grab some of those large duffel bags too, buddy. I'll focus on gear while you get that stuff loaded up."

Fortunately Ben had completed doing his big spring inventory a couple weeks ago and just finished restocking pretty much everything in the store the day before their fishing trip. This was the routine every year in anticipation of the summer tourist season.

There would be no tourist season this year in Durango, or anywhere for that matter, Ben thought. Not for a long time to come.

· 13 ·

Before Ben grabbed himself a replacement knife, he pulled the tactical rifle case with the AR-15 inside from under the rear seat. Wanting to make sure it didn't get covered, he slid it between the passenger's seat and the center console for the time being.

Turning his attention to the shelves behind him and a box with a Spyderco label on it, he pulled out a smaller box and unceremoniously pulled a new knife out of its case. He opened it immediately and zipped it across the top of a box full of headlamps. He grabbed several with his hands, took a step toward the truck and tossed them into the back.

He repeated this process with the box of knives, and just about every other box on the shelves. Methodically, he made his way around the room taking a few of some things and all he had of others, like the replacement filters for the water purifier. Fighting his urge to grab it all, he tried to be conscientious of the steadily dwindling space they had remaining in the truck.

"Now what?" Joel stuffed the last of six heavy duty canvas duffel bags alongside the cube of white tubs he had built in the back of the truck.

"Pretty much anything you think we'll need. Even if we already have it at the house, it doesn't hurt to have backup. You never know. How about extra fuel canisters for the stove? Might as well grab a few extra stoves while you're next to them," Ben suggested.

The Titanium Ultra-Light camp stoves were made to handle a small pot. It was ideal for two people and small enough to fit in the palm of your hand.

Most of the items Ben carried in his store were made for backpacking and backcountry camping. Everything was designed to be as small and as lightweight as possible for extended backcountry trips. This allowed them the benefit of getting a lot of 'bang for the buck,' as Ben would call it, out of the space in the truck. They would be set up for a long time and wouldn't have to worry about provisions too much on the way to Ocean City if they were conservative. If the roads were anything like what they had seen so far, it would be a long trip. But they should have enough. Worst case scenario, they would have to do a little hunting and fishing to make it last, but they would definitely have to pack the truck below the window line. He didn't want to advertise their abundance of resources and good fortune. That type of thing could get you into a lot of trouble fast.

Ben stepped back, contemplating as he glanced back and forth from the loaded down truck to the remaining boxes on the shelves to see if there was anything else they should grab or try to fit into the truck.

"I think that just about does it, Joel." Ben walked over to the steel security door that divided the storefront from where they were and peered through the peephole.

"I just want to look and see if my old revolver is still there or if it disappeared along with everything else up front," Ben whispered as he continued looking through the tiny hole in the door. "I want you to wait here though, in the back. Okay?" He turned to look at Joel.

"Yeah, okay," Joel answered. "Dad, do you mind if I put together a bag of extra stuff for Allie and her Mom? They might need it, and if we're just going to leave the rest here... I'll carry the bag on my lap."

"Actually, I think that's a great idea, Joel. As a matter of fact, I was going to offer to leave one of those tubs of dehydrated food with them, if you want. We have plenty for just the two of us if we supplement with hunting and fishing when we can.

I have more at the house, not to mention, half a box of MREs."

"Okay. Thanks, Dad." Joel nodded.

Joel darted off towards the shelves to look for a suitable bag as Ben watched him for a moment, proud of his son for being so thoughtful at a time like this. He must really like this girl, Ben thought to himself.

He refocused his right eye and looked through the peephole again, checking to make sure it was still clear before he unlocked the heavy-duty deadbolt. The key turned with a *thunk*, and he slowly eased the door open just far enough to slip through.

He put the keys in his pocket using his right hand and brought the gun back up from its holster all in one movement while keeping his left hand on the door. He closed the door behind himself as he slipped into the room and considered locking it for Joel's sake, but decided to leave it unlocked and closed in case he had to make a hasty retreat. Besides, if he left the door open it might attract attention from the street side if someone were to walk by. Ben was sure that looters would return at some point and finish what they had started, eventually gaining access to the rear storeroom.

He crouched down, balancing on his feet, and shuffled over behind a display rack that had been full of merchandise the last time he'd laid eyes on it. He made his way over toward the counter where the register used to be, now nothing but a few wires remained protruding from the countertop in its place. They had literally taken everything that wasn't fastened down and even some things that were. Of course the glass case that had displayed the handheld GPS units, high-end fly reels, watches, and knives was shattered and empty. Ben shook his head in disgust, half the stuff looters had taken wouldn't even work, thanks to the EMP. It just served as a reminder of the type of people who were responsible for this. There was no thought put into this, pure reactionary panic. It must have been every man for himself.

There was glass everywhere, and he was trying to be careful as he laid the Glock down beside him. He reached under the register counter feeling with his fingers, as he went for the hidden compartment under the register where he kept an old .38 snub nose revolver. After the break-in he'd started keeping it there as an extra precaution. He slid the small wooden door on the compartment open and reached inside. For a second, he thought they'd gotten the gun too.

"Got it," Ben whispered to himself, pulling the gun out along with a small box of ammo that he kept with it. He tucked the .38 into his rear waistband and picked the Glock back up.

The truth was Ben didn't care that much about

the old pistol and was surprised it was actually still there. He had better guns at home in the safe and plenty of ammunition for them. He was actually considering leaving the gun with Allie and her mom, depending on the situation when they found them.

The real reason Ben wanted to have a look around the store was to get one last look at what he had worked so hard for and perhaps also to get some kind of closure. It had taken everything he had to open the place ten years ago. It had provided for his family and, in the beginning, it had given him a real sense of purpose after the Army.

The Army had taught Ben a lot, and he had excelled through the ranks, but it had also left him burned out and apathetic. Every deployment began to look the same—the same people, the same problems, and the same objectives. He had lost a couple of friends along the way, and the mileage had begun to take its toll on him. He'd decided to abandon his Army career aspirations after only twelve years in and rejoin civilian life while he felt he still could.

He'd had a harder time than he anticipated adjusting to so-called normal life and floundered for a while. He'd tried college for a couple of years, but all it left him with was a little student debt and a desire to get away from most of the people that he'd met there.

He lucked into a gig as a fly fishing guide through a friend at school, and it rekindled a passion in him that he hadn't felt since he was a kid. Ben found himself spending more and more time camping and fly fishing in the back country when he could. He enjoyed the solitude and felt like that was where he belonged. That is, until the winter that he'd met Casey, and that changed everything for Ben.

She was attending the local college and finishing up her nursing degree when they first met at a mutual friend's holiday party. They hit it off immediately and seemed to fill a void in each other's lives at the time. They moved in together within a few months. Needing something a little more stable than guiding to raise a family, Ben had decided to open the store. It had allowed him to still be involved in the things he loved and make an income as well, so he'd considered it a fair compromise.

Later on, when their marriage hit tough times, it had been his only place of refuge. He'd even slept there a few times towards the end of the marriage. After they'd separated and eventually divorced, it had given him a reason to get out of bed in the morning and get on with his life.

Other than the kids, whom his ex had tried to keep from him at the beginning of the separation, the store was all he had. It had been good to him and now, all those years were gone.

Looking around now in total disgust at what was left of it, Ben began to come to terms with the fact that this may be the last time he ever saw the place.

· 14 ·

Resigning himself to accept the fate of the store, his thoughts were interrupted by the familiar yet unwanted sound of a car exhaust echoing off the storefronts on Main Street.

"Crap," Ben muttered, mad at himself for even thinking about retrieving the gun now. He thought about making a break for the door but the car sounded close, and he didn't want to risk giving away their position. Best thing to do is stay put, he thought. They'll probably just drive by, nothing left in here to steal anyway. Ben glanced back at the door.

"God, please let Joel listen to me for once in his life, and stay in the back like I asked," Ben whispered to himself.

He was worried that Joel would open the door to look if he heard another car, and Ben didn't want to be seen until he was sure of their intentions.

Ben turned his attention back to the street as he

put one knee down and stabilized himself from his crouched position behind the counter. He peered around the edge of the counter and, thanks to the cleared-out store, had a pretty good view of the street from where he was.

Shifting the Glock slightly in his hand, he watched as an old blue Chevy El Camino crept into view. Two younger guys sat low in the front seat. The passenger's tattoo-covered arm was hanging partway out of the window with a cigar between his fingers.

Ben knew the type, unfortunately, and had seen Durango change a lot in the past ten years or so. The big city life had crept in with every transient move to the once small town. The same people fleeing that urban life for the tranquility of Durango had ironically brought it with them.

Gangs weren't a big problem in town, but with the legalization of marijuana, the harder drugs seemed to find their way into town as well, and the gangs seemed to follow. They had grown in numbers the last few years, but usually kept to the west side and rarely ventured downtown. The Durango he had known was changing rapidly, and he didn't like it.

As the car came into full view, Ben could see that it had been heavily modified with big gaudy rims and what he guessed was a lowering kit of some type. The car looked like it would get hung up on a speed bump. He always wondered what the fascination was with lowering a vehicle. Not that it mattered. As long as they kept on moving past the store he would be happy. The deep, sparkly, blue paint glistened in the early morning sun as the car rolled by painfully slowly.

"Come on, keep going, keep going, that's it," Ben whispered to himself.

It seemed to take forever to move beyond the storefront. When just the back end of the car was visible, Ben began to rise slowly to his feet but froze when the car abruptly came to a stop. Ben returned to his previous crouched position and cursed under his breath as he watched impatiently.

The car backed up until he could see everything but the front of it and stopped once more. He could see the two men talking to each other but couldn't make out what any of the conversation was about over the sound of the modified exhaust. Just then, the engine went silent, and the two got out of the car.

Leaving the El Camino's doors wide open, they casually sauntered toward the busted up storefront. The driver had a patchy beard and was slightly taller than the passenger, who sported a red bandana around his head. Both were covered in tattoos.

Ben had a couple of tattoos that he'd gotten while in the Army. He and some of the guys from his regiment had decided to ink themselves after a particularly grueling deployment that had seen them lose a couple close friends. He earned his tattoos, and they meant something to him.

These guys were covered in what was probably meaningless ink that was all for show, and it made him dislike them even more.

Now they were standing just outside on the sidewalk, and Ben could clearly see that they each had a pistol tucked into the waistband of their pants. Broken glass crackled under their feet as they talked.

"Man, I told you we got everything from this place. There ain't nothing left here," the driver said, making jerky movements with his hands.

"What about the back? There's gotta be some stuff in the back." The passenger uncrossed his arms and stepped through one of the broken front windows of the shop. He got his baggy pants stuck on some pieces of broken glass sticking out of the sill, causing him to hop on one foot for a second, trying to regain his balance.

"You're wasting your time, man. We tried that door, but we couldn't get it open. That's why I said we need a chain or somethin' to hook to the car and yank it off its hinges." The driver shook his head and laughed at his friend's clumsiness. "Come on. There's other places to hit, better places!"

His amusement turned to frustration quickly as

he turned back to the car without wasting any time waiting for his passenger.

"Well, wait up, man!" The guy in the store threw up his arms and hobbled over the windowsill again, not faring much better than he did on his first attempt. Shouting some profanities at the driver, he ran to catch up and join him in the car.

Ben heard the engine start up, and he immediately felt a sense of relief, knowing that one of the many scenarios playing out in his mind wasn't going to happen. They were going to leave without incident.

The passenger barely made it into the car before it started rolling away from the storefront. When Ben was satisfied that they were indeed leaving this time, he made for the door promptly. As he got close, he noticed that the store side of the door was full of dents and all scratched up around the lock. In fact, the lever style lock had a slight outward curve to it where someone had no doubt tried to pry it open with a crow bar. Now seeing this, he was surprised the door still worked.

"Money well spent." He re-holstered his gun as he pulled the door closed behind him and locked the deadbolt once again.

"Did you see any of that?" Ben looked at Joel.

"I saw them." Joel nodded. "They didn't look too friendly."

"What gave it away? Was it the guns, or the fact that they were returning to the scene of the crime?" Ben said sarcastically.

"Were they the ones that did all that?" Joel asked looking back in the direction of the storefront.

"Them and their friends. One of them mentioned trying to break down that door when they were here the last time, and they're coming back to try again," Ben said.

"When?" Joel eyed the door.

"I don't know, but we're leaving now," Ben said. "Finish putting that bag together for your girlfriend and let's go. They can have the rest of this crap. It doesn't matter anymore. We got the important stuff anyway."

"Not my girlfriend!" Joel said as he stuffed a few more things into the bulging duffel bag. "We're just friends, I don't even know her that well."

"Sorry. You know what I mean." Ben rolled his eyes and patted Joel's shoulder. "Hey, leave room in there for this." He handed Joel the .38 and the box of bullets for it.

"You sure?" Joel asked.

"Yeah, I mean if they need it. We sure don't." Ben shrugged.

"Nice. Thanks, Dad!"

Ben walked over to the rear door on the building

that led to the alley and stopped to listen for any sound. Satisfied that no one was in the alley, he unlocked the door and cracked it open enough to look out. Scanning the alley from one end to the other, he didn't see anything.

"We're good. I'll get the door. You pull the truck out." Ben closed the door and locked it. He knew looters would eventually break into the shop and take the rest of the stuff, but that didn't mean he had to make it easy on them.

Besides, it would keep the thugs busy while he and Joel put some distance between them and the downtown area. Assuming that they didn't run into more thugs on the way out of here.

Joel managed to find a spot on the back seat for the extra bag he'd made up and, after he finished cramming it in, he climbed behind the wheel and waited for his dad to make his way around to the big roll-up door. Ben threw the bolt on the door and slowly lifted the door. Moving the door up slowly again so as not to make any more noise than necessary.

Joel fired up the engine as the door rose above the hood and eased the truck out into the alley once the door was high enough. Ben hurried to get the door down opting to go with speed over stealth at this point. Now that the big V-8 was echoing off the nearby buildings in the narrow alley, there was little point in being quiet.

Ben quickly attached the chain and padlock that normally secured the big door from the inside. Without looking back he ran around to the driver's side door. Joel had already opened the door and slid over to the passenger seat.

"Good job, bud. Now, let's get out of here."

· 15 ·

"So, what was that address?" Ben asked.

"401 East Seventh Street," Joel replied. "Not very far from here."

"That's good, the less time we spend in town the better. I'm sure those two guys aren't the only two riding around. It's obviously 'every man for himself,' by the looks of things." Ben's gaze lingered on yet another burned-out vehicle.

Had the EMP somehow generated a powerful enough pulse to cause overheating in computer controlled devices and electronics causing fires? Was that even possible? That wasn't the first car they had passed that was burned to a crisp, seemingly without any interaction with anything else. They'd passed plenty of burned-out cars that had apparently collided with a building, a tree, a sign, another car or something. But some of the burned-up wrecks they saw were alone in the middle of the street.

The worst part about the car wrecks they passed were the people that had been trapped inside or were too injured to drag themselves away. Ben knew Joel was seeing these things too. He hadn't said anything to Ben about it, but Ben knew Joel saw them.

The twisted, half-charred remains partially protruding from windshields were hard to miss. How long would they be left that way, Ben wondered? Caught in their final moments with no one to help them?

Without the usual emergency services and government infrastructure rushing in to clean up the gory details of these events, there would be no filter on their world anymore. People, including his son, would be exposed to the raw harsh reality of things. Joel was going to have to grow up fast, and Ben hoped he was up to it.

"It's really pretty bad, isn't it?" Joel shifted in his seat. "I mean, I... I didn't expect all this."

"Well, it isn't good that's for sure. I had no idea things would fall apart this fast, and you know, without police, fire and EMS, there's no one to help. This might not be the best place for your friend Allie and her mom to stay."

Ben immediately regretted saying that last part out loud, he hadn't thought that far ahead yet, at least when it came to the girl and her mother. What if they needed help? He didn't want any distractions right now. Besides he had his hands full with taking care of Joel and trying to get to his kids in Maryland. He had to stay focused. The trip would be hard enough for him and Joel, not to mention having Gunner along. There wouldn't even be enough room in the truck for all of them.

Ben kept coming up with excuses in his head as to why he couldn't get involved with two other lives right now, but he knew in his gut that he also couldn't leave a teenage girl and her mother to fend for themselves in this grim reality. Maybe they wouldn't even be there, or maybe they had left town when things turned for the worst like so many others appeared to have done. Whatever situation he and Joel encountered when they got there, they would have to make some hard decisions and make them fast so they could keep moving. He wanted to get on the road to Ocean City as soon as they could.

"So, tell me what do you know about this girl and her mom?" Ben asked.

"Not very much. I mean, I've had some classes with her, but I don't really know her that well. She moved here during the last school year. From Pittsburgh, I think, with her mom.

"Oh, I thought you didn't know her very well," Ben teased, trying to lighten the mood.

"Well, I meant, that's all I know, so…" Joel said.

"I'm just giving you a hard time, bud."

"I know." Joel shook his head. "Hey, don't miss the turn. Left here."

Ben steered left onto East Seventh Street and drove toward the residential section of the street which was still a few blocks away. This part of East Seventh was still considered downtown and was mostly made up of small businesses, like Ben's store. He could see this area hadn't fared much better than Main Street and most of the shop windows were busted out here as well. As they neared the area of single family homes located at the end of the street, Joel began counting off the house numbers as they passed.

"395… 397… 399, should be the next one." Ben grabbed Joel's knee with his right hand and squeezed it firmly. His posture straightened as he gripped the wheel with the other hand.

"There they are!"

· 16 ·

"Who? Where?" Joel looked around.

"The guys from the store." Ben nodded. "Up ahead, it's them."

Up ahead about 150 yards away, sat the blue Chevy El Camino. It was parked across the sidewalk and backed into the front yard of a house down the street but on the opposite side Allie's house was on.

"Great," Ben muttered. "Is this her house?"

"That's her blue Jeep." Joel pointed.

Ben turned sharply, catching Joel off guard, causing him to lean into the console and grab the door handle.

"Whoa," Joel shouted.

"Sorry, needed to get off the road fast. Those two are bad news." Ben put his hand on Joel's shoulder and helped him back upright as he whipped the Blazer in on the far side of the driveway next to Allie's Jeep. The Jeep was small next to their truck and didn't do a great job of blocking them from sight. Ben hoped they were back far enough off the road that the two thieves wouldn't notice the addition of their truck to the street.

"Looks like they're cleaning that place out." Joel looked at the El Camino, its rear bed full of household items.

"Yeah, it's a shame," Ben said. "Let's hope the owners are long gone." He didn't doubt for one minute that they were dangerous and should be regarded as a serious threat. He wasn't about to underestimate the danger the two thugs posed and their potential to cause serious problems.

"Okay. Here's the plan. I'm going to find a spot on the front porch and camp out with the AR. You go around the side and look for another entrance. Hopefully you can get someone to answer the door, but there's a good chance they're gone, Joel."

"I know," Joel mumbled.

"Whatever you do, don't walk around to the front of the house. If nobody answers just come back to the truck and wait for me. We can't be here long, so we won't be able to wait for them if no one's home. Okay, buddy?"

"I understand." With that, Joel eased open the passenger door and slid out, heading down the side of the house.

Ben opened his door and got out, then leaned back in and pulled the rifle bag out by its strap.

Keeping an eye on the El Camino, he made his way up onto the front porch.

The house was a modest little Arts & Crafts style bungalow with a big covered front porch. Large oversized columns lined the perimeter of the porch and one on each side of the front steps with a railing connecting them all. The columns consisted of a stone base about three feet tall and almost as wide, on top of each stone square sat a wooden post completing the connection up to the roof.

Ben crouched down behind the right-hand column and laid the bag in front of him. Unzipping the bag the rest of the way, he pulled out the sleek matte black AR. Then he pulled a collapsible bipod out of one of the accessory pouches on the bag, slid it onto the key mod style rail and tightened it near the end of the grip.

Extending the bipod feet he lay down in a prone position around the side of the column, pushing the gun in front of him until he was lined up behind the scope. He flipped down the magnifier and zeroed in on the car first and then scanned the window for any sign of movement.

He wondered how Joel was making out and hoped he wouldn't take it too hard if they came up empty here today.

Joel followed the narrow gray flagstone sidewalk around to the back side of the house where it ended at a set of small steps that led up to a door set back into a small landing area. Joel cleared the first two steps in a single stride but stopped dead in his tracks when he reached the third.

The door was ajar and sat open, but only by a few inches. He climbed the last few steps cautiously until he reached the small wooden landing. Tilting his head at an angle he pushed his right eye to the opening. He tried to look into the house through the crack between the door and the jamb but couldn't see much of anything.

He knocked on the door lightly, although he wasn't sure why at this point, and immediately regretted doing so as the door creaked on its rusty hinges and swung in a couple more inches.

"Well, that was smart," he whispered to himself.

Joel stood motionless for a second, wondering what his next move should be. Should he go and get his dad? No, he said not to go into the front yard. Maybe just take a quick look inside and see if anyone was home. He wanted to handle this on his own anyway.

Could it be that they'd left in such a hurry, they hadn't even bothered to close the door much less lock it? Maybe they were gone and he would never see Allie again. Pushing the negative thoughts out of his mind, he nudged the door open a little more to peek inside. Cringing, as the old hinges gave him away with their metallic squeals, he peered around the door.

The place was trashed, and it wasn't Allie and her mom bugging out kind of trashed. Things were broken and furniture tipped over. The place had been torn apart by looters, maybe the two idiots down the street had been here too.

Then he noticed the inside of the doorjamb. It had been forced open and was reduced to splinters by some sort of blunt force from the outside.

Joel's heart raced as his mind tried to make sense of it all. Had they been home when the house was broken into? Was Allie okay?

"Allie?" Joel called in as loud a voice as he dared. "Allie, are you here? It's me, Joel!"

No response.

"Please, God, let Allie be okay. I'll never ask for another thing as long as I live. I can't handle two in one day," he whispered to himself.

· 17 ·

Joel found himself pushing further past the door into the house. Even though his mind was telling him to stop, his legs seemed to have a mind of their own.

He pulled out the 9MM pistol and held it firmly in his right hand. His palm was sweaty, and he squeezed the gun extra tight to compensate for his shakiness. He brought his other hand up to the gun to steady his grip as he held it at shoulder height in front of him. He tried to remember what his dad had taught him about how to clear a room and approach corners.

He and his dad were regulars down at the shooting range, and he had always enjoyed going there and shooting the different guns they owned. The range had a couple different competition pistol courses that local law enforcement used to train. When the pistol courses weren't in use, they were open to any member of the range to use. Joel and his dad had taken advantage of those opportunities and run the courses many times. It was one of his favorite things to do there, and he'd gotten pretty good at it over the years.

Now he just had to put it all to use in a real world environment.

He brought his trembling hand up to wipe away a bead of sweat that tickled his face as it ran down from his forehead, then quickly put his hand back on the gun.

Real life was a lot different than the range when the potential targets that could pop out at any second from behind the next corner weren't made of paper. It all seemed like a lot to think about at the moment and he had to force himself to refocus on the task at hand and settle down a little before he continued.

Swallowing hard, he made his way forward putting most of his weight on the balls of his feet, selecting each step carefully. He moved through the kitchen where he'd entered the house to what looked like a dining room.

The china cabinet lay face down at an angle where it came to rest on the dining room table and the spilled contents were all over the floor in broken pieces. Trying not to step on any of the glass or china pieces, he tactfully tiptoed through the room without making a sound.

Up ahead appeared to be the living room with a

set of stairs on the right. The steps went to a landing and then turned back in his direction and rose out of sight. In the middle of the room was the front door. The porch where his dad was set up must be beyond that.

He briefly considered opening the door and letting his dad know what was going on, but decided against that for fear of blowing his dad's cover and giving away his location. Joel was probably already in trouble for coming in here alone.

He went over to the bottom of the stairs and looked up. There was a small hallway at the top, but he could only see a few feet in either direction.

"Allie?" he called again, a little louder than the first time and with a little more confidence. Joel was pretty sure the house was empty at this point, and his hopes of finding Allie were fading fast.

He thought about going upstairs, and even climbed a few steps, but instantly had second thoughts. The house wasn't that big, and he was sure someone would have heard him by now, not to mention, he had already been in there for too long and was probably in for a lecture from his dad, as it was.

"Allie?" he called one final time before he turned around and headed down the stairs, now with his gun held loosely at his side in one hand.

As he stepped off the last stair tread, he heard a faint voice and spun around.

"Joel? Joel Davis, is…is that you?"

Joel felt the blood rush to his head and a feeling of warmth flooded over him. Forgetting all about caution and proper protocol, he quickly ran up the stairs and looked down the hall to his left and then to his right.

"It's me. It's Joel. Allie is that you? Where are you?"

"I'm in here, the bedroom on the right, at the end of the hallway," Allie answered, her voice still sounded muffled, like she was in the wall or something. Joel jogged down the hall making sure to holster his gun, which he now just realized still had the safety engaged. How stupid I am, he thought. I wouldn't have been ready if I had needed it.

"Gotta do better," he mumbled.

Now in the room, he still couldn't see her. Had he gone the wrong way? Then he heard a noise from inside a large walk-in closet. He turned to see two legs dangling from a small attic access in the ceiling.

He rushed over to the closet, as she slid the rest of the way through the hole. She all but landed on him. Joel caught her before she hit the floor and helped her get her balance before he let her go. But Allie hung on to Joel for a second longer. He didn't object.

"Are you okay?" he asked.

"I think so." Allie reluctantly released her grip on him and backed away a few inches. He could see that she had been crying.

She glanced toward the stairs. "We have to get out of here, Joel. Before they come back."

"Who?" Joel asked.

"Those guys, whoever they are. They're the ones that made this mess!" Allie looked around the room. "Wait how did you get here? I've been trying to start my car since yesterday and its dead… everything is dead!"

With that, she hung her head and began cry into her hands.

"What's wrong? Allie? Talk to me." Joel bent down a little and tried to look her in the eyes.

"My mom. I haven't seen her since before the bombs or whatever they were that hit us. I'm scared that she may be… I think she's…" Allie choked on the last few words and couldn't get them out as she teared up again.

"Hey, I'm sure she's fine. We can help you find her," Joel offered, as he put his hands on her shoulders.

"You don't understand. Joel, my mom is a flight attendant. She was in the air when it happened." Allie closed her eyes and sighed deeply, fighting back yet another wave of tears.

The gravity of the situation struck Joel like a ton of bricks, and he knew, just like Allie knew, that her mom wasn't coming back. She leaned into Joel again, and this time he readily embraced her as she released a torrent of pent-up emotions.

Joel didn't know what to say at first and then thought it was best not to say anything at all. It felt good to hold Allie, and for a moment, he forgot about everything as he inhaled the flowery sweet smell of her hair. This certainly wasn't the way he pictured this happening, and he hated to see her hurt so badly. He knew he had to do something. Anything. There was really only one thing he could do for her right now.

"You're coming with us." Joel pulled away a bit and looked down at her while trying to make eye contact. She rubbed at her eyes and looked up at him.

"Really? Are you sure?" Allie asked.

"Yes! Absolutely! You can't stay here. I won't leave you here." Joel doubled down on his promise.

He suddenly felt an overwhelming sense of responsibility as the words of his offer played over again in his head.

"Who's we?" Allie asked.

"My dad," Joel said. "He's on your front porch right now, keeping an eye on those two idiots that are ripping people off. They're down the street a few houses right now, by the way, so we really should get moving."

"That's what I was going to tell you before. If it's

a blue car then, yeah, those are the same guys that broke in here. There was an older pickup truck with them too. I think there are about four or five of them. They've been terrorizing the neighborhood or at least what's left of it. I heard a few gunshots across the street last night and when I looked out the window, I saw them walking over to my house. I wasn't sure what to do, so I ran upstairs and hid in the closet, but when I heard them kick the door in, I climbed up into the attic and closed the hatch behind me. I could hear them talking when they were in the house and overheard them say they would be back later, so I've pretty much been up there ever since. Except for a few times when I came down to try to start my Jeep or find something to eat and drink." Allie took a big breath after getting her story out, still wiping the tears from her eyes.

"Oh, wow. I am so sorry! Let's get you out of here," Joel said, trying to encourage her into moving faster.

It felt like it had been a while since he entered the house, and he was now extremely anxious to get back outside and get going. His dad was probably freaking out right about now, on how long he was taking.

"We have plenty of supplies from my dad's store, so really all you need are clothes and a good pair of hiking boots. Pack light."

Joel added the last part, thinking this might buy him some favor with his dad. The last thing he wanted to do was break the news to him that Allie and her five suitcases were coming with them. He was sure his dad would see it his way—he had to. They couldn't just leave her here to fend for herself.

Maybe he was worrying for nothing, and his dad would be fine with it. After all, he was the one that had said, 'this might not be the best place for your friend Allie and her mom to stay,' on the ride here.

Deciding not to waste any more time worrying about it, Joel focused on helping Allie get her things together so they could leave.

Allie led Joel down to the other end of the hallway and into her room. She opened the bi-fold doors on her closet and tossed him a purple duffel bag that read Durango Demons Field Hockey on the front. He recognized the bag from the times he'd seen her practicing after school when he had been there for lacrosse practice.

"Is that too big?" Allie asked.

"No. I think it's good." Joel laid the bag on the bed and spread it open. She began throwing things into the bag almost immediately. Joel looked around the room and noticed a few ribbons and trophies on a tall blue dresser by the door. There was a picture on the dresser of Allie and an older man, maybe her father, Joel thought.

Meanwhile, Allie had darted back out into the hallway and returned in less than thirty seconds with a variety of things from the bathroom. Running over to the bed she let them spill out of her arms into the open duffel bag.

"That's my dad," she said. "He lives in Pittsburgh."

"Wow! Really? Huh." Joel's eyes widened. "My mom lives in Maryland with my brother and sister. I don't really talk to her all that much though, mostly just my brother and sister."

"We usually talk once a week or so. I don't have any siblings though."

Allie stuffed a few final pieces of clothing into the bag and looked around the room for a second. She scooted over to the dresser and opened the top drawer on the dresser and stuck her hand into the back corner rooting around for something. With a slight grin and a sigh she pulled out a small leather-bound notebook with a couple hair ties wrapped around it. The little book was stuffed full and well worn with bits of paper sticking out here and there.

She held it to her chest briefly and smiled, then stuffed it into her bag and zipped it closed. The smile was gone as quickly as it had appeared. Allie grabbed her bag and turned to Joel.

"I'm ready."

· 18 ·

Joel led the way down the steps with Allie right behind him. He was about to offer to take the bag for her when all of a sudden, a loud *POP—POP* broke the silence.

Joel hunched his head down in a knee-jerk reaction as Allie jumped back and let out a shriek.

"What was that?" She grabbed at Joel's shoulder.

Before Joel could answer there was a more distant *bang—bang*, then the AR reported three more times *POP— POP—POP*!

They were almost at the bottom of the steps now, and they could see the muzzle flashes through the front window. The thin curtains barely concealed the flares of light that flickered in unison with the loud crack of the rifle.

"Dad, are you hurt?" Joel shouted in the direction of the front porch hoping his dad could hear him through the wall.

"Negative. Meet me at the truck. Double time." Joel heard his Dad's no-nonsense reply faintly through the wall.

"This way, quick!" Joel grabbed Allie's hand and pulled her in the direction of the back door. Stumbling through the house they made their way through the wrecked dining room, trampling on dishes and kicking furniture out of their way as they went. They continued their hasty exit through the kitchen until they reached the back door. Joel almost yanked the door open to bolt out of the house with Allison, but stopped himself, thinking to check first and make sure it was clear.

Slow down. Got to think. He pulled the 9MM out again and slowly opened the door using the tip of the gun. Grabbing the duffel bag handle closest to him with his left hand he took half the weight from Allie so they could move faster.

"Here, let me help you," he said.

"Thanks." She took the opposite handle as he led them out the door and down the steps. Joel scanned their surroundings for danger as they ran clumsily with the big duffel bag. They slowed down as they approached the corner of the house, and Joel carefully peeked around before they continued to the truck. He could see his dad already at the truck, crouched down behind the front of the truck with the AR laid out on the hood trained towards the street.

Joel holstered his pistol, relieved to see his dad.

"It's okay. Come on." Joel turned and looked at Allie.

Now out in the light of day, he noticed how pale and weak she looked. The poor girl. Who knew how long she'd been stuck up in the attic? He grabbed the other handle from Allie and took the entire weight of the bag from her.

"Let me get that for you, okay?" With a quick lunge, he hiked the bag onto his shoulder and headed for the truck.

"I can help," Allie protested as she followed him.

"It's no problem, really, let me help you," Joel said without breaking stride. "It's the least I can do."

Joel let the bag slide to the ground from his shoulder and crouched down behind the hood next to his dad with Allie falling in behind him. "What happened?"

"Our friends decided to pay us a little visit and wouldn't leave well enough alone." Ben continued watching the street before turning to look at Joel and then Allie.

"Hi there, you must be Allie. I'm Ben." He extended his hand.

"Hi." Allie shook his hand.

"Sorry to have to meet you under these circumstances, Allie. Are either one of you hurt?"

"No, we're okay." Joel spoke for the both of them.

"So, is it just you or is there anyone else?" Ben looked at Allie.

Joel tried to intercept his Dad's gaze and shook his head bleakly, hoping his dad would pick up on his cue and leave it at that. He turned to Allie and put his hand on her shoulder and then looked back at his dad.

"Okay then. If you have everything, let's get out of here. No need to meet their friends." Ben nodded his head at the street. "You guys will have to squeeze in on that side somewhere. Joel, see if you can make that bag work and find Allie a safe spot to sit." With that, Ben snatched the AR off the hood of the truck and smoothly folded the bipod legs back against the rail. He slid it barrel first into the rifle bag leaving only the butt of the gun sticking out. Walking around and opening the driver's door he wedged the bag with the gun tip down between his seat and the center console making the rifle easy to access.

Joel stared at the loaded truck for a second or two and decided to not even waste his time trying to get the bag to fit. Wrestling the bag to his shoulder again, and then over his head he gave it a final heave onto the roof of the truck where it landed between the Thule crossbars of his roof rack. Then he took the extra bag he had packed for Allie from the store out of the truck and threw it up there as well. Reaching under the passenger's seat he pulled out a couple tie downs and lashed the bags to the rack.

This opened up a tight spot in the middle of the rear bench seat for Allie, and she crammed herself in between the gear and sunk down out of sight from outside the truck.

With everybody and all their gear squeezed into place, Ben fired up the truck and backed out of the driveway. Once they were out on the street, Joel had a better view of the front yard turned battlefield.

The El Camino's engine was sputtering as it labored to remain at idle. The car had come to an abrupt stop colliding head first into a utility pole at the edge of the yard. The front bumper was badly dented but otherwise the car looked okay. Joel could see the driver slouched over the steering wheel, the front windshield cracked in a weblike pattern radiating out from two separate bullet holes. The passenger was a few yards away laid out on the street behind the car. His legs and arms extended outward in an awkward pose. He was still holding a gun in his right hand and was lying in a pool of blood that had started to run toward the storm drain in the street.

When they were even with the El Camino, Ben threw the truck into park and hopped out leaving the door open.

"Wait here one second," Ben ordered.

"What are…?" But his dad was already walking away.

"What's going on?" Allie couldn't see very much from where she was seated in the back of the truck and was walled-in by gear.

"I'm not sure, but my dad is smart with this kind of stuff, so there must be a reason for whatever he's doing."

Joel watched as his dad went straight to the driver and pushed his limp body over onto the passenger seat, and reaching in, he turned the car off and popped the hood.

"What do you mean by that?" Allie tilted her head still trying to catch a glimpse of the action.

"He used to be an Army Ranger." Joel looked back at her. "We're in good hands."

Joel watched his dad as he pulled the keys out of the car's ignition and threw them into the bushes. Then he proceeded to walk around to the front of the car and open the hood. Reaching into the engine compartment he pulled out a fist full of wires and threw them on the ground. Without skipping a beat, he produced the knife from his pocket and punctured both front tires.

Joel had never seen his dad move like this, with such purpose. Maybe a little at the range or on the pistol course, but this was different. The look on his face was all business and reminded Joel that he really didn't know that much about what his dad had done in the Army. Sure he knew he was a Ranger and had heard a few mild stories about some of his dad's adventures, but he'd always felt like Dad was holding back on some of the details. Now he was sure of it as he watched his dad cleanly move about.

"That ought to keep them busy for a little bit." Ben climbed back into the truck as quickly as he'd gotten out, and before Joel had a chance to process it, they were speeding down the street headed home.

"So what happened back there while we were inside?" Joel asked.

"They finished up at the house up the street and were headed back down East Seventh. I guess they noticed our truck. The driver already had his gun out the window as they pulled into the yard." Ben paused for a minute as he steered the truck around a wrecked car in the road.

"I couldn't take any chances, Joel. There was no choice really. Those guys were looking for one thing only. There would have been no reasoning with them, and they would have killed us all to get their hands on this truck and our gear."

"I found her hiding in the attic from them. They were the same guys that broke into her house and destroyed the place. She said there were more of them yesterday when they came around." Joel looked back at Allie and saw that she was fast asleep wedged between the bags.

"I'm sure she's exhausted." Ben glanced back at her. "We can't go back there to her house, to town, any of it, for a long time," Ben said.

"She knows. She doesn't have anything to go back to anyways." Joel checked on Allie to make sure she was still sleeping. "Her mom is… *was,* a flight attendant. She thinks she was in the air when it happened." Joel looked down at the floor and then back at Allie again.

"Does she have any other family around here?" Ben asked.

"I don't think so. Just a dad in Pittsburgh is all I know of." Joel shrugged.

"Pittsburgh, huh?" Ben gave Joel a look.

"What?" Joel protested.

"Nothing, just don't get any ideas. The three of us need to sit down and discuss all our options after we get home and get settled. Your brother and sister are my top priority, along with you, of course." Ben reached over and tousled Joel's hair as he shot him a crooked smile.

"I know, but we can't leave her on her own." Joel blushed and turned away to look out the window.

"I know, bud, I wasn't saying that. We just have to work out the details is all." Ben put his other hand back on the wheel and stretched his neck to one side then the other.

"Thanks, Dad," Joel said.

"Thanks for what?" Ben asked.

"Everything." Joel managed a small grin and shifted lower in his seat. He put his elbow on the door and propped his head up with his hand as he stared out the window, letting his thoughts take over.

What a day it had been. It was only midafternoon, but he felt like it should have been much later. He'd had to come to accept the loss of Brian, his best friend, and assume the role of protector for the girl of his dreams who was now sleeping in the back of his truck.

The loss plus the new responsibility combined with what they had experienced in town was enough to leave his head spinning.

All things considered, the day could have turned out much worse. He had no idea what tomorrow would bring, but he was sure of a few things.

He had his dad, he had Allie, and they were headed home.

· 19 ·

Ben had taken a different way home for a couple reasons, the main one being to avoid driving back through town and running the risk of meeting up with any more undesirables. The other reason he wanted to head out of town on Rt. 160 was to get a better feel for how the bigger main roads were as far as obstacles and wrecked vehicles. It was a longer route home already and with the amount of accidents on the road it ended up taking them close to an hour and a half to get back to the house.

Allie slept the whole way back, even the last mile or so up the bumpy dirt road to their house. Ben felt relieved to pull into the driveway, but wasn't about to let his guard down.

"Wait in the truck for just a minute, okay, bud? Let me just do a quick walk around." Ben turned off the engine and hopped out. Everything appeared to be as they'd left it, but after the day they'd had, he wasn't just going to assume all was well. He checked the doors on the garage first to see that they were still locked, then walked around the house doing a visual check on doors and windows. He caught a glimpse of Gunner inside, at a couple of the windows, pushing the curtains aside in his excitement and slobbering up the glass. This brought a little smile to Ben's face, and he was glad to see that silly dog.

Satisfied that it was all clear, he called to Joel from the front porch. "All right, why don't you guys come on in? Don't bother with any of the gear other than Allie's things. I want to unload all of it in the garage and sort through it there."

"Okay." Joel turned to Allie and paused for a second before he woke her. She looked so peaceful tucked in amongst the bags. He wished he could let her sleep and enjoy her alternative reality as it was surely better than this one they had.

"Allie… Allie, we're here." Joel gently shook her knee. "Hey, we're here."

She rubbed the palms of her hands into her eyes as she finally came to.

"Where are we? How long was I asleep?" She yawned.

"We're here, at our house. You slept the whole way. About an hour and a half." Joel grinned.

"I did?"

"Yep. You feel a little better?" Joel wished he hadn't said that immediately after it came out. Of course she didn't feel any better, she had just lost everything, including her mom.

"Yeah, maybe a little, I guess. Although I feel like I could fall right back asleep." She managed a brief smile.

"Come on, let me help you out of there." Joel offered his hand.

She had sunk even further down into the gear on the ride back and now her knees were almost at her head level. She grabbed Joel's hand with both of hers, and he pulled her out of the hole. Once out of the truck and standing on her own two feet, she stretched and took in her surroundings.

"Wow, nice view up here. You guys are pretty high up, huh?" Allie said.

"Yeah, right around nine thousand feet. Really great sunsets up here." Joel nodded in the direction of the currently sinking sun.

"Yeah, I bet. Just you and your dad live here?" Allie asked.

"Yep. Whoa, there. Look out. Don't worry, he's friendly." Joel barely dodged Gunner as he came barreling down the steps and flew by him heading straight for Allie. Joel was worried she would be intimidated by Gunner's exuberance, not to mention he probably almost weighed as much as she did. But he was pleasantly surprised when Allie dropped to her knee to greet the big beast of a dog.

"Hey there, what's your name big boy?" She fawned all over him, rubbing behind his ears briskly. Gunner leaned into her and almost knocked her over before she caught herself.

"And that would be Gunner." Joel chuckled. "Sorry about that, he doesn't know how big he is."

"Oh, it's okay. I love dogs! We have a yellow lab named Molly who lives at my Dad's."

"Okay, Gunner. Give the girl a break." Ben walked back out onto the deck from inside the house where he had done a quick walkthrough, making sure it was secure.

"He'll let you scratch him all day you know." Ben smiled and shook his head at Gunner. "Joel, why don't you help Allie get her bag inside and show her to the newer bathroom downstairs? It's nice and clean and has a good size tub that I bet she would love to put to use."

Allies eyes lit up when Ben mentioned the bath.

"I'll get the generator going so you'll have plenty of hot water."

"Wow, thank you so much, Mr. Davis," Allie said. "That sounds wonderful."

"After you show her around the place, Joel, how about giving me a hand in the garage unloading the truck? Then, maybe after that, we can all sit down and get to know each other a little better over a hot meal." Ben nodded at Allie and headed for the garage, pulling the keys out of his pocket.

"Sure thing, I'll be right there." Joel pulled at the bag on top of the truck until it slid off onto his shoulder with a *thunk*. "Right this way, ma'am." He led Allie up the stairs and into the house with Gunner closely trailing after his newly found friend. He took her to the bathroom downstairs and turned the tub faucet on, letting it run until he felt warm water.

"Well, there you go, enjoy." Joel began to back out of the bathroom, pulling the door closed behind him.

"Joel, wait."

"Yeah?" he stuck his head around the partially closed door.

"Thank you, for today, for everything. If you hadn't come looking for me, well I don't know what I would have done," Allie confessed.

"You don't have to thank me. I'm just glad you're okay." Joel looked down at the floor.

Without warning she leaned in and kissed his cheek then pushed the door closed. Stunned, Joel was left standing outside the bathroom door. He turned around to see Gunner staring up at him.

"What are you looking at?" Joel cleared his throat and headed back up the steps. He left the door open at the top of the stairs for Allie's sake and turned to wait for the dog, but Gunner was still at the bottom of the stairs sitting by the bathroom door.

"Well, are you coming?" Joel looked at Gunner who responded by lying down outside the door with a grunt.

"Traitor," Joel teased. "Fine then, stay there."

When he got to the garage, his dad had already backed the truck in and was unloading gear.

"You okay?" Ben asked. "You look a little red."

"Yeah, I'm fine, just a little worn out I guess." Joel still felt the lingering effects of the warm flush that had crept across his face just moments ago. "Need some help?" He tried to shift the focus off himself.

"Yeah, let's get all this stuff out of the truck and lay it on the floor over there so I can get it organized." Ben pointed to a clear spot on the floor next to the truck. "So, how's she doing?" Ben asked.

"Okay, I guess," Joel answered.

"She's been through a lot. We all have. So just make sure you give her time to process all that's happened, and just be there for her, even if all you do is listen." Ben glanced at Joel as he passed him the white food tubs from the back of the truck.

"I'll try." Joel paused. "I can't imagine how she feels. We're all she's got now. I mean, except for her Dad in Pittsburgh."

Ben slid the last white tub out to the tailgate from the cargo area and stopped to look at Joel. "I just want to make sure she's up for the trip. It won't be easy, so she has to be onboard one hundred percent. She might not want to leave Durango."

"I don't see why she would want to stay. She's got nothing left here," Joel said.

"What if her dad comes looking for her here? I don't know. Let's get her take on all of this at dinner. Here you go." Ben tossed three dehydrated meal packets at Joel from one of the tubs. "How about boiling up some water for us inside so we can eat soon? I'll finish unloading and join you in a minute."

"Okay." Joel wanted to continue the conversation but didn't want to push it, so he headed for the house instead.

Even so, he knew there was no way he was leaving Allie behind.

· 20 ·

Ben finished unloading the truck and had even started to organize the gear when he noticed it beginning to get dark out. He stopped what he was doing and closed the garage doors, locking everything up as he went.

When he entered the house he could smell the food, and he was quickly reminded how hungry he was. Other than the granola bar this morning and a Clif Bar he'd shared with Joel on the ride home, he hadn't had a thing all day.

He noticed the kitchen table was all set up with glasses of water for everyone and plastic silverware with paper plates laid out all in their proper places. The setting was complete with a candle in the middle to top it off.

"Who are you, and what have you done with my son?" Ben smirked as he looked at Joel.

"What? I just set the table, and the candle is so we don't have to use the lights," Joel reasoned. Just then Allie came up the stairs in new clothes and looking much better than before.

"Smells good, can I help?" she asked.

"Not much to do really, just add water and wait." Joel finished pouring the boiling water into the bag and closed the top. He brought the bags to the table and set one in front of each plate.

"I see you've made a friend." Ben watched Gunner as he followed Allie to the table.

"Yes, I think so too." She looked down at Gunner and smiled. "Oh it feels so good to be clean," she said and sat down to the table.

"So, Joel tells me your dad lives in Pittsburgh?" Ben pulled out a chair and sat down at the end of the table.

"Yeah, I was going to visit at the end of the summer for a couple of weeks." Allie fidgeted with her plastic utensils.

"Any other family or relatives around here? Anybody you could stay with?" Ben asked.

"No, it was just me and my mom here. I have some other relatives in Pittsburgh also, but I don't really know them that well."

"Do you think your dad will try to come and get you here?" Ben leaned back in his chair rubbing the three-day-old stubble now covering his face.

"Well, I wish I could say yes, but the truth is, probably not. He doesn't even have a car because he works and lives in the city so he really has no use for one. I don't know how he would even get here." Allie shrugged. "Um… Joel told me that you guys are going to Maryland to get his brother and sister. Is that true?" She perked up in her seat a little.

"Yeah, that's the plan. I was hoping to leave by mid-morning tomorrow." Ben massaged the bag of food, trying to mix it together and speed up the rehydrating process. "I want to go through most of the gear tonight and try to pack the truck a little. Maybe finish up with a few odds and ends in the morning and then get going."

"Dad, we have that old Thule rocket box under the porch. I could clean it up in the morning and mount it to the roof rack. It would make a lot more room inside the truck." Joel poked at the bag of food in front of his plate. Joel's angle with the rooftop cargo box was obvious to Ben, and he gave him a knowing look.

Ben didn't like the idea of doing anything that might hinder getting to Bradley and Emma, and he certainly didn't want to get sidetracked God knows where in Pittsburgh. This trip would be complicated enough.

On the other hand he would never be able to look Joel in the eyes again without feeling guilty if they left Allie behind. If they let her stay here at their house, the supplies would eventually run out, and it just wasn't sustainable long term. Even with what they had, he'd already figured that he and Joel were going to have to supplement their food rations with wild game when and where they could.

Even if running out of food wasn't a problem, the type of trouble that they had run into today in town would eventually make its way to the outlying communities, including Durango Hills. He knew that Allie's fate here, if left alone, would be grim at best.

"Is this what you want to do, Allie? It could be pretty tough going out there on the road." Ben now looking directly at her.

"He's all I have left." She spoke softly as her eyes began to water and turn red.

Ben could hear the desperation in her voice as he stared at the young woman in front of him who was only a few years older than his own daughter. He leaned in to the table and reached out his arms putting one hand on Joel's shoulder and the other on Allie's.

"We'll get you to your dad," Ben stated.

"Thank you so much!" Allie jumped up from her seat and hugged Ben.

"Thanks, Dad. I'll get the box mounted on the truck first thing in the morning." Joel leaned in, unable to hide his excitement.

After they finished eating, Joel excused himself and took a shower, giving Ben and Allie a little time to sit and talk. In the short conversation they had, Ben realized what a bright, articulate girl she was. She seemed mature beyond her years and, by the end of the conversation, Ben was confident he had made the right choice to bring her along. Maybe with Allie around, it would push Joel to be more responsible.

Joel came downstairs from his shower and joined the conversation for a few minutes before Ben decided he better get started going through the gear. Finishing the last sip of his coffee he stood up from his chair.

"Well, I'm going to try to make a dent in organizing the truck. Joel, show Allie to the guest room, okay?"

"Yep," Joel said.

"Oh, and you might want to light a few more candles. I'm going to kill the generator when I go out. Don't stay up too late, guys. Tomorrow is going to be another big day," Ben warned.

"I won't be up much longer that's for sure." Allie stretched and yawned, waking Gunner who was curled up next to her on the couch.

"Good night, then." Ben headed outside, leaving the two teens inside to their conversation.

As he wandered out onto the deck, he paused for a minute and looked up at the stars while he rubbed his neck. What had he gotten himself into? Trekking across the country with two teenagers in a post-apocalyptic world?

He didn't know what they would find, but it was sure to be the challenge of a lifetime.

Find out about Bruno Miller's next book by signing up for his newsletter:
http://brunomillerauthor.com/sign-up/

No spam, no junk, just news (sales, freebies, and releases). Scouts honor.

Enjoy the book?
Help the series grow by telling a friend about it
and taking the time to leave a review.

ABOUT THE AUTHOR

BRUNO MILLER is the author of the Dark Road series. He's a military vet who likes to spend his downtime hanging out with his wife and kids, or getting in some range time. He believes in being prepared for any situation.

http://brunomillerauthor.com/

https://www.facebook.com/BrunoMillerAuthor/

Made in the USA
Monee, IL
08 December 2021

84344973R00095